YELLOW DOG

It was during a dark thunderstorm that young Eddie Riner fired his .36 Whitney Colt at the domineering rancher Bur Blackrule and then ran to the mountains. Six years later, on his return to Yellow Dog, Eddie learns from a doctor's inquest that another gun must have been fired on that fateful night. Hiding his true identity, he accepts the role of deputy marshal. But only with the help of a saloon girl and a tough trail finder can he finally uncover the truth behind Blackrule's killing and mete out grim justice . . .

Books by Caleb Rand
in the Linford Western Library:

THE EVIL STAR
WOLF MEAT

CALEB RAND

YELLOW DOG

Complete and Unabridged

LINFORD
Leicester

First published in Great Britain in 2002 by
Robert Hale Limited
London

First Linford Edition
published 2004
by arrangement with
Robert Hale Limited
London

The moral right of the author
has been asserted

British Library CIP Data

Rand, Caleb
 Yellow dog.—Large print ed.—
 Linford western library
 1. Western stories
 2. Large type books
 I. Title
 823.9′14 [F]

ISBN 1–84395–201–7

Published by
F. A. Thorpe (Publishing)
Anstey, Leicestershire

Set by Words & Graphics Ltd.
Anstey, Leicestershire
Printed and bound in Great Britain by
T. J. International Ltd., Padstow, Cornwall

This book is printed on acid-free paper

1

The Night Shoot

Following the gunshot, the thick-set body of Bur Blackrule tumbled from the porch steps. It rolled heavily down the treads to the gummy mud of the yard below. Driving rain washed away the blood that welled from the middle of his broad chest.

A few moments later a girl ran into the open doorway of the ranch house. She was silhouetted by the yellow light behind her as she stared in disbelief at the body. She swallowed a horror-struck scream.

Across the yard, the rain lashed down on the thin form of a youngster who stood with razor-cropped hair and tattered bib overalls. In the brilliance of a jagged lightning flash, the girl saw he was gripping the butt of an old revolver.

He appeared to be rooted to the spot, ankle-deep in the clutch of the mud.

A storm gust caught the open door of the ranch house and slammed it to. The light from the inside lamps vanished and the girl shrieked in the sudden blackness. She ran down the water-soaked steps, stumbled across Blackrule towards the shimmer of light from the bunkhouse windows. Water was sluicing from the overhanging roof, splattered a small, broken wood-framed mirror under her feet.

Eddie Riner stood open-mouthed, numb with shock as the girl stumbled past him. He looked from Blackrule's body to the gun now hanging limp from his hand. He shook his head in disbelief of what had happened. 'No, no,' he said in a panicky whisper. 'I ain't killed him.'

Raised voices from the bunkhouse warned him, brought him round. He gasped, as another lightning bolt cracked open the night. He saw the ghostly faces of the Fat B cowboys as they piled into the yard.

Bare-footed, he turned and ran, swung behind the broad bole of a live oak. Gasping and trembling, he watched the yard and the ranch buildings. More lightning slashed down, and he saw the men through the heavy curtain of rain. He saw them crowd around Blackrule, heard the harsh voice of Bo Horselip, the foreman.

'You see who did this, Miss Katey?' he called out.

'I saw Eddie Riner. He was standing . . . just standing . . . ' Katey Cate's words trailed off. Her hair was plastered to her pale wet face as she walked through the rain, pointing to the edge of the yard.

'The dough-gut.' Horselip snarled. 'Go get him, boys.'

Eddie Riner heard the command. He knew all the names, the tags they afforded him. Most were to do with his being an orphan and he didn't wait to hear any more. He'd run for the shelter of a barn, back of the ranch house. He'd have to chance the open, being revealed to the ranch hands by flashes of lightning.

After a wild dash, he threw himself behind a brimming water-trough, then between the bars of a pole corral. He scrambled to his feet and stared breathlessly around him. There were no horses — the corral was empty. He pushed his revolver into his bib pocket, thought for a moment before picking up a lariat coil. Ahead of the storm, the Fat B's saddle stock had been turned out to the home pasture, and a grim smile twitched at Edson's face.

He ran again, vaulted the far side of the corral, and made for the pasture. Behind him, he could just hear the shouts and curses of the men who were setting out after him.

When he reached the home-pasture gate, his chest was heaving and the storm ran into his tears of anguish. But thunder had started rolling towards the distant peaks of the Raft River Mountains. The night turned even blacker and Edson unbent from the dying storm.

Under the last flash of lightning he saw the horse herd. It was bunched in a corner of the pasture, rumps solid to the driving weather. He pushed the gate wide, ran for the wet, gleaming coats. He worked the lariat, slipped a running noose over the head of a grey as it turned towards him. He swung up on the nervous animal and reined it across the pasture. He yelled, kicked its belly as the rest of the cavvy broke in terrified flight.

Already spooked by the thunder and lightning the horses were in a mood to run. They raced through the gate with Eddie flicking and tugging at his grey's improvised headstall. Within minutes, the Fat B saddle stock were no more than a distant rumble of hoofs. The punchers had been trapped at the ranch by Eddie's desperate breakout.

★　★　★

Ma Gracey lived in a rough loggers' cabin in the timberline of the Rafters — as the Raft River Mountains were dubbed by folk along Snake Plain. In between tending her small family of waifs and strays, she made lace charms and dolls that she peddled in the Yellow and Grey Dog towns, sometimes to the small homesteads that fed off Goose Creek.

It was past midnight and the storm was a distant murmur when Eddie urged his hard-blowing mount through a breach in the rocky wall. Under the dripping trees he slid to the soft ground and slipped the headstall, slapped the grey across its rump.

Without a sound he walked barefoot towards the darkened cabin. The door sagged on a broken hinge, scraped the floor as he pushed it open. He flinched, stood hesitant in the doorway.

'That you, Eddie?' came a strained, worried voice.

'You better hope it is, Ma,' he replied. 'You must be soaked to the skin.

Where you been?'

'I been down at the ranch killin' a man, Ma.'

'You been . . . done what?' Her voice was still touchy, anxious. She hadn't fully realized what Eddie had said.

A light flared in the darkness. Eddie blinked, watched the flickering match held high. Ma touched a tallow lamp then moved towards him, saw his tense, defiant features.

'You killed a man, Eddie? Is that what you said?'

'Yeah, Ma. Reckon I shot Mr Blackrule.'

'Bur Blackrule? Oh Eddie, what you gone an' done?'

'He came at me with a quirt. I only went to give Miss Katey one o' them little purses. She's leavin' for St. Louis. You told me men ain't for whippin' Ma.'

'I did Eddie, an' I meant every word.' She trembled. 'What you shoot him with? That ol' smoke pole you carry around.'

'I never meant to kill him, Ma. That's the truth.'

'I know it, boy. The trouble is, I'm goin' to be the only one who does.'

'Yeah. I guess we always get the hot end o' the iron,' he said acidly. 'There's no 'fraidy hole, Ma. If I don't get away, they'll string me up.'

Ma wrung her hands. 'If it had been anyone but Mr. Blackrule — '

'They'd probably only broke my bones,' Eddie cut in. 'I'm real sorry, Ma. Fat B's the biggest spread west of Falls Lake. Blackrule's punchers'll run you an' little Birdy off the plain, for what I done. They been waitin' for somethin' like this.'

'I'll get you somethin to eat,' she said dully. 'Shuck them wet clothes . . . an' take your hat.'

While Birdy slept and Ma Gracey folded some biscuits, dry fruit and cheese into the corner of a gunny sack, Eddie changed his clothing. Carefully he checked and wiped dry his .36 Whitney revolver.

The sky was peppered with stars now, while the swollen river eased itself through Snake Plain. Ma Gracey quietly appeared in the cabin doorway and held out Eddie's scant provisions.

'Where you headed?' she asked, the words catching in her throat.

'Back up through the trees into the mountains . . . then east maybe.' Eddie sniffed, twisted his bony fingers in the folds of Ma's dress. They won't catch me,' he said manfully. 'I'll come back . . . one day.'

Ma had no more words, she just swallowed and bit her lip. Knowing she'd never see Eddie again, she stood and watched him climb for the timberline. She stayed until he disappeared in the crystal starlight that followed the storm.

★ ★ ★

Far off, hidden in the dense pine, Eddie stopped and turned. He looked east of Goose Creek, wondered if it was the lights of Fat B he saw. At sun-up he guessed they'd have rounded up their horses, and hit his trail. But by then he'd be where no rider would reach him. Climbing steadily on, his bare feet hardened against cone and rock shale, his mind twisted and prodded at Blackrule's death. With the Whitney he could knock a gopher back into its hole at twenty paces. Yet at half that distance, he'd fired at the ground in front of Blackrule and shot him dead. He'd been rattled for sure, but the shakes never got to him that bad.

2

Leaving Home

High above Eddie Riner, ragged pinnacles thrust into the mighty Nevada sky; Snake Plain rolled out like a map at his feet. Stretched on an outcrop of the Rafters, the rising sun beat off the rocks, warmed him through the thin cambric of his shirt. To the south curved the willow-lined Snake River. The wide running water was silted, deeply coloured from the storm and had breached its banks.

In between, and dwarfed by distance, were the Fat B ranch buildings. At a 20 degree angle to the west, lay Mose Rizzle's Rolling Post ranch. Between the two spreads, willow and birch marked the freshet windings of Goose Creek. Further to the north, the low, rocky trail of the stage line was just visible as it scratched a route through the shimmer of Yellow Dog and Grey Dog, Eddie Riner held up his slouch hat, scanned the familiar land. He knew that any Fat B rider on his trail would ride him down like a mustang runner.

Bur Blackrule was a powerful man, but there wouldn't be a run of tears at his death; Eddie knew that. The Fat B boss had always ridden roughshod over anyone who opposed him. His wealth and brutal influence made him impervious to county law. The man had assumed the role of Katherine Cate's guardian when her folks had died in the smallpox outbreak of ten years back. But Blackrule was wifeless, and locals claimed Katey was a surrogate daughter, another ornate collectable for the big ranch house.

As she'd grown, Blackrule forbade her to leave the ranch. He didn't allow her into town even. Ma Gracey had laughed at that. She said it could be the only decent thing he'd ever done. Katey was unhappy, but she'd had a ready smile for Eddie, the cute looking boy who came down from the hills with a good line in doodads. They were visits Blackrule wouldn't tolerate, though. 'Mountain peddlers' he called such folk, the sort he'd bring out his whip for.

Suddenly Eddie tensed. He squinted, drew in air through his clenched teeth. Sunlight had glinted off a rifle barrel or telescope below him. He whispered irritably, as he saw the rising dust from a group of riders beating up the slopes towards the timber. Behind them, way out on the plain, a second bunch of horsemen were circling the Rolling Post ranch. That would be Marshal Purle Briscoe, with a posse of towns-men.

Getting to his feet, Eddie grasped the gunny sack and began to climb. He couldn't give the chasing men time to work their way around him. It would take them hours, but on foot he needed time to get beyond the trees. It was an unyielding wall of rock that separated

13

the timberline from the mountains proper and Squirrel Gap was five miles to the west. There were narrow clefts through which Ma Gracey and horsemen in the know could ride, but they were unknown to Bo Horselip, or the marshal and his posse.

★　★　★

It was first dark when Briscoe's weary posse trotted their mounts back into Grey Dog. The marshal was a heavy, middle-aged man, and it was plain he felt his years as he slumped in his office chair. There had been a time when Purle Briscoe was a no-nonsense lawman. He'd kicked hard, but those days were long gone.

He heard the jingle of spurs, looked up tiredly to see the rough-hewn features of Bo Horselip step through the doorway.

The Fat B foreman grunted, stood waiting for the marshal to speak.

'Any sign?' Briscoe enquired of him.

'Nothin'. Not even his dung,' Horse-lip growled.

'Didn't expect anythin' else. The kid got more'n eight hours start, an' he knows every snake trail through that goddamn treeline. None of us got a chance to trail him up there.'

'Yeah, well, I'm takin' my boys through the rimrock at sun-up. We'll find Squirrel Gap. You comin'?'

'Nope,' Briscoe said. 'An' the county ain't payin' three dollars a day for any man to choke on his dust, either,' he added.

'We're talkin' murder an' you have a duty,' Horselip pointed out bluntly.

'I know it, an I'm sendin' word to Cole Morelock. He'll put out a dodger. Between here an' Boise, some lawman'll pick Riner up.

Horselip sniffed disdainfully. 'We'll ride,' he said.

Briscoe sensed more than impatience in the Fat B foreman. 'Anyways', he said, 'I reckon you . . . we been firin' off a mite soon. If I'm goin' to get a report out, I need to know the full rights o' the killin'. Tell me about it.'

Explaining wasn't Horselip's long suit, and for a brief moment he considered his words before he spoke. 'Er, accordin' to Miss Kate, seems like Riner had brought her a little board mirror. It was a gift on account of her leavin' for school in St Louis . . . seems he was sweet on her. Well, Purle, you know how old Bur felt about young bulls sniffin' around his prize possession.'

Briscoe nodded. 'Yeah,' he said with obvious distaste. 'I do know. I know he took some skin off young Jago Rizzle a month back. Gave him a real hidin' for gettin' too close. You goin' to tell me the same thing happened to Riner?'

'Sounds like maybe, yeah. The kid must've said too much. Bur caught him an' broke the doodad apart . . . questioned Riner's family line. The kid backed off across the yard, but Bur crowded him . . . showed him the quirt. Riner pulled his old hogleg . . . proved

16

it weren't as useless as some thought'

Briscoe licked the tip of a pencil stub, started to write on a sheet of paper. 'The girl ... Katey,' he said impatiently. 'She told you all this? an' you reckon it weren't self-defence?'

'I reckon it was murder.'

'Yeah, I thought you would,' agreed the marshal. 'How'd you rate this for a description? EDDIE RINER. WANTED FOR SNAKE RIVER MURDER. AGE BETWEEN 14–17. SHORT FAIR HAIR. GREY EYES. NO OBVIOUS SCARS OR MARKS. CARRIES AN OLD WHITNEY COLT,' he read.

Briscoe didn't wait for Horselip to answer him. He eased himself from his chair, pushed past the Fat B foreman to stand in the doorway of his office. He scanned the foothills above and below the rimrock, up to the peaks of the distant Rafters. 'Not that any o' that matters,' he said with an almost detectable trace of pleasure. 'We seen the last o' that boy, believe me.'

3

Back To The Dogs

The River Stage Line, between Idaho Falls and Boise, was officially for mail, but it frequently carried a ragbag of frontiersmen, most of them fully armed and headstrong.

As new veins of gold and silver were discovered in mountain ranges north of the Snake River, the eastwest advance increased, and banditry got its reward. Stagecoaches were frequently held up and occupants robbed, sometimes killed. For the outlaws it meant easy pickings; swollen grain pokes from those who had struck it rich, and cash and valuables from the affluent cattlemen. Drivers were reluctant to make the cross-country journeys, and were hard to come by.

In the Snake River town of Pocatello,

a miner and two land speculators destined for the border town of Payette had waited two days for the through stage. But a rider had brought in news of more outlaw activity and they were prepared to wait another day before going on. They voiced their fears to the driver, and suggested the stage company take on more buckshot men as an effective defence.

'You take it up with 'em. I'm paid to take this coach out at noon, an' that's what I aim to do,' the driver responded confidently.

There were no ready takers for the ride, and the stage was filled with dry goods and army provision boxes. There was a man in a long buckskin coat however, who'd decided to make the journey, and the driver said he'd have to make his own space. Edson Ringer nodded his acceptance, showed his Boise ticket.

'You'll have yourself some company as far as Glenns Ferry,' the driver said, as a small, dapper, dark-suited man

19

walked up. It was Rumer Wheat, the sutler, who was carrying profitable goods for the soldiers of Fort Denton.

One of the men who wasn't going called for Ringer and Wheat to rethink their journey. 'There's no witnesses to real bravery,' he shouted.

'If the driver reckons he can make it, I'll take my chances alongside him,' Ringer answered back.

'That's what we need . . . someone with little imagination,' Wheat said to the driver as the fearful passengers departed.

Ringer muttered something under his breath as they climbed aboard the stage. The sutler rode alongside the driver as reluctant shotgun, and Ringer wedged himself among the pile of trade.

The driver pulled out his old stem-winder, gave it a few winds. He checked the time, grunted approval. 'Near enough,' he confirmed. He gathered up the reins and let loose the handbrake, shouted for the team to move off.

Except for one overnight stop-over, there were no comfortable halts along the dog-legged route, just coldharbour relays. Between these stations the stage rolled along at good speed, the changes usually made in less than fifteen minutes.

As they approached the first of two scheduled stops before Glenns Ferry, Rumer Wheat got more anxious, less keen on his profit from the army.

'We got no real reason to stop at either o' these dog holes,' he said. 'Take us on . . . go through.'

'Goes well with me,' the driver shouted. 'An' I've heard them sister towns called worse.'

From inside the coach, Ringer heard. He pulled his hat down over a fleeting, secretive grin.

For two further hours the stage rollicked along its route. The horses were enjoying the pull as they approached a shallow creek that wasn't far from the trouble-spot of a week before.

'Look to your guns, sutler,' said the driver. 'If anything happens, don't do too much talkin'. Start shootin'.'

Ringer poked his head out of the stage window. 'How 'bout me, driver?'

The driver winked at Wheat. 'That's encouragin',' he said. 'A wolf in sheep's clothin'. Pick 'em up, girls,' he then shouted, but the horses shied, bucked in their stride. Off the trail, they'd seen a coyote pack. The ferocious dogs snapped and snarled as they dragged at bones and meat. It was where one of the horses from the attacked stage had met its end.

'That's where they took the stage,' the driver remarked, as they jounced through at speed. He looked uneasily around him.

'You reckon we're on our own out here?' Wheat asked.

'Cain't tell,' the driver said thoughtfully. 'Cain't tell.'

Hognose Pass was a few miles further

west. It was on the second part of the dog-leg, and the trail ran between low rock formations that wound along the side of the river.

It was early evening as the stage slowed in its approach to the pass. Heat was still rising from the ground, but in the shimmer mounted riders were visible from a quarter-mile out.

Wheat spoke nervously to the driver. 'There, ahead.'

The driver never flinched, or took his eyes off the trail ahead. 'I seen 'em. Hold tight.' He gripped the reins, and sent the team into a full gallop.

★   ★   ★

From the saddle of his big chestnut horse, Bramwell Mace gripped his Winchester. The polished steel barrel glimmered in the first dark, and he ran his thumb against the breech-block. He raised his left hand to shield his eyes, and watched the stage as it lurched into a sudden clip for the pass. He shook his

23

head, turned to Quinlan and spoke slowly.

'He's whippin' the horses. They're going to race through.' He pointed into the low, undulating rocks. 'Use the ground, clefts, mesquite as cover. Shoot the lead horse.' Quinlan looked critical, but Mace responded quickly.

'No other way. Keep the men quiet. Move now.'

As Quinlan swung away, Mace held in his mount, squinted at the approaching stage. It was close enough now for him to see the faces of the two who rode on top. He heard a short, sharp whistle. It meant that Quinlan was well hidden, and positioned with his rifle. Mace looked around him, satisfied. Apart from a whiptail that skittered from its hiding place, he couldn't see any unnatural sign, and he stepped his horse a pace forward. He spat a thin stream of tobacco juice, then he was gone; expertly fusing with the shapes and textures that edged the pass.

★　★　★

The stage creaked and rattled wildly in it's headlong dash. The horses were still fresh and strong, and they thrust their glistening heads forward. The driver was calling for more effort, cracking his whip, when one of the lead pair suddenly slewed, buckled into a dive against its partner. It was fractionally after the unmistakable crack of a rifle from up ahead.

Wheat and Ringer were ready. They fired simultaneously from the stage, but it was into thin air. As they took the first twist in the pass, the riders had withdrawn into the low, layered rocks.

The dying animal had brought the stage to a halt, and the driver was staring wildly about him. He sprang from the box, and ran to cut free the harness. The horse had taken a fatal bullet; its hind legs jerked, and its neck arched in its last few seconds of life.

It was then that the hold-up men appeared from cover. They were firing revolvers and rifles, but they held off from the stage because Wheat and Ringer were again measuring out a barrage of gunfire. The driver yelled curses at Mace's men and grabbed for his pistol. He flung himself low across the dead horse, emptied his cylinder into the gang.

Wheat and Ringer continued their fire and brought down two of the men. The outlaws were checked and whirled their horses, once again disappeared into the bleak landscape.

'Now cut him loose,' shouted Wheat, grabbing up the reins again.

But the driver didn't move. He lay still and silent across the broad belly of the dead horse. The remaining horses were stamping the ground in alarm. Ringer climbed from the stage, and Wheat handed him down the reins. The sutler leaped to the ground, and ran with his head down. The driver had been hit twice, and was already dead.

Ringer walked up, his breath coming in short, excited spasms.

Wheat rose to his feet, and took a long look at the distant mountains.

'He was a brave driver. One day these outlaws are gonna' get hit real bad for all this.' He grasped the driver by his leather jerkin, pulled him into the stage, and laid him across his supply boxes.

Ringer cut loose the dead horse. He tied its lead partner on behind, and flung the front harness around the next pair.

Wheat was sitting ready to move off, and he looked sharply at Ringer as he climbed up beside him. 'You want to go on?'

'A lot more'n I want to go back,' Ringer said, gripping the shotgun.

'Yeah, that sure is a town on the black road.' Wheat blew air through his teeth, and looked across the heads of the pulling horses. 'But right now, you ain't got much of a say in which way we're headed.'

The stage had been quickly and stealthily surrounded by half a dozen hold-up men. They'd changed their tactics, sat their horses, threatening and silent.

'Goddammit,' Ringer yelled. 'I wanted a choice.' He swung up the shotgun, leaped to his feet, and fired both barrels out at the men. Wheat cursed, and made a grab for his big revolver. Mace and his men were momentarily stunned by the explosive retaliation, and those nearest to the stage were being bucked in the saddle.

Ringer's hat had flown from his head, and the assailants saw his uncut hair as it fell to his shoulders. Their reaction was immediately faltering, and there was no doubt in Rumer Wheat's mind that they were thinking as he was. Ringer's blue breeches only added to the illusion.

'Inside,' Wheat yelled, and they both rolled off their seats, throwing their legs and bodies into opposite sides of the stage. They knew they weren't going anywhere, and in fear and defiance they piled more fire out of the windows. 'Get the boxes around you,' he said, shoving the driver down to the floor of the stage. They lay in silence for five minutes before the sutler decided to have a look out. He squeezed himself across to the other side of the stage. There was nothing to be seen, except the settling dust from the outlaws' horses.

'They've gone, kid. Gone for real this time.'

Ringer eased himself into a corner of the stage, his feet avoiding the body of the driver. 'How'd we know that?'

'Because they don't think it's *you*, kid. They think you're someone else. Remember most of that scum are army deserters . . . an' desperate. We've just seen that. They'll skin you for less than a han'ful o' coin.'

'What's that got to do with me?'

'Nothin' except they think you're *General George Armstrong Custer*. I know he's a long ways from here, but believe me, *you're him*. As long as there's a tune from a fiddle, they won't be back.'

Ringer knew that Wheat was partly right and laughed nervously. 'Can't think what Custer would be doin' sittin' in a pile o' candy. But I guess these brave runaways are nervy enough to believe anythin'.'

'Yeah, an' ruthless too. We'll lay up here, and wait for the next stage to pass.' Wheat looked nervously at Ringer, noticed a trickle of blood from the sleeve of his skin jacket. 'You're hit.'

'Yep, but it don't hurt much. It's done more damage to your beads 'n blankets than it's done to me.'

It was nearly full dark when they heard the approaching stage. It was down from Boise, and heading towards them. As he brought his team through the pass, the driver swerved and pulled up alongside. He immediately advised Ringer to go back.

'There's some folk with a taste for buckshee army stock. You best move out fast,' he said.

The man who rode shotgun with the incoming stage squinted at Ringer, made a double take on his appearance, then agreed to transfer. But Wheat's eagerness for profit won out. He'd pay a substantial kick-back to the incoming driver, get his supplies to the night stop.

Ringer sat atop the returning stage, and looked down as the sutler walked towards him.

Wheat held his hand up, smiled wearily. 'I have to go on, you understand,' he said and smiled broadly. 'It's been a pleasure meeting you. I maybe got you wrong when we started off . . . underestimated you. Maybe next time we meet, I'll stand you a drink, eh, General?'

'Yep, maybe.' Ringer gave a lean smile, shook the man's hand.

The coach would be attempting a fast return to Idaho Falls, avoiding many stops on route. But a few miles from where Goose Creek joined with the Snake River, Edson Ringer would step down, make his crucial, fateful return.

4

Grey Dog

It was just after noon, when the ill-fated River Stage pulled up alongside a willow brake, outside of Grey Dog.

'Good luck,' the driver called out as he pulled away. 'Looks like you're goin' to need it.'

Standing alone, gripping his meagre traps, Edson Ringer looked around him. Nothing seemed to have changed much in the six years he'd been away. That was the last time he'd seen the town. That was when he'd been Eddie Riner — the leppy mountain kid who'd shot and killed Bur Blackrule.

'I never wanted to come back,' he explained to the scrawny cur that pressed its jowls into the dirt in front of him. 'Not ever.'

But the dog wasn't getting involved.

It huffed, lifted its leg with disdain then slunk away.

A massive heat shrouded the town. At the hitch rail fronting the Low Lamp saloon, three horses and a mule switched restlessly at the swarming flies. A razorback hog pushed its snout into the dank garbage that clogged the alley alongside.

Edson pressed against swing doors, edged his way into the saloon. He gulped at the press of fetid air, the clamour of raised voices. He kept his eyes ahead, made for the crowded long bar. He blinked against the heavy curl of tobacco smoke and ordered himself a beer. Then he found a seat at a table, sat with his back against a rough, mud-chinked wall.

No one paid him any attention, and after a few minutes he risked a searching look around him. He looked for a sign of recollection in any of the faces, but all he saw was the red blotch of heat and too much drink. There were no memories from the past other than those he carried in his own head.

Edson had finished his beer, was contemplating the slide of froth on the inside of his empty glass when the saloon doors were pushed violently aside. A sudden chill hit the room, closed down the rumble of talk.

Then Edson recoiled, swore as the crash of a gunshot reverberated in the confines of the room. He pushed the palm of his right hand against the butt of his Colt, raised his eyes. The man was thin and narrow-shouldered, dragged a twisted leg. He was of similar age to Edson himself, but that's where the similarity ended. This one was carrying a chip on his shoulder for being as he was. Under his breath, Edson called him a name, watched him push a Colt back into his cross-draw rig. But he was a little late and the man saw his lips move, made eye contact.

'What was that, mister?' he asked in a curious croaky murmur. 'Looked like you was sayin' somethin'.'

Edson shook his head and smiled

thinly. 'No,' he said, realizing the man was already drunk.

'You was probably thankin' me for buyin' you a drink,' the man goaded. Then he swung around and tossed a clinking pouch onto the bar. He waved clumsily at the bemused patrons. 'That'll buy juice for you scum to suck up,' he told them.

The men shuffled uncertainly, until one of them shouted, 'He means, 'free beers'.' Then they crowded tight to the bar and the man looked back to Edson. His face broke into an unpleasant grin.

'Hey General,' he yelled, laughing at his joke. 'You get up now and join them wooshers, you hear.'

'I'm finished drinkin' . . . was about to leave,' Edson drawled.

'Look around you, General. They know somethin' you obviously don't. Like, when I say drink, you drink.'

Edson gave a tolerant smile. He was going to say that the only person ever to order him to drink was Ma Gracey, and that would have been a spoonful of

35

molasses for his own good. But he settled for a more rousing stance.

'When I came in here there was somethin' nosin' around the alley,' he said. 'It looked as though it could be kin o' yours. Now why don't you go an' spend some time with it . . . leave the likes o' me alone.'

The man nodded. He thought for a second or two, then began to laugh nervously as he took in Edson's proposition. Being insulted in public was something that didn't happen to him too often, and never in the Low Lamp saloon. Men standing close suddenly shuffled away. They were clearing the lines of fire, distancing themselves from what was about to happen. The man sucked in air noisily, retreated a step as the anger surged. He looked around him, grinned spitefully then came back, slammed the flat of his right hand on Edson's table.

'Goddamn you soldier boy,' he rasped, making a move for his Colt with his left hand.

He was fast, but Edson was ready; had been ever since the man pushed his way through the saloon doors. Edson slammed his beer glass down onto the man's knuckles, simultaneously brought up his revolver. He came out of his seat, swung the gun hard and fast in a rising loop until it connected with the man's twisted face.

'I ain't a soldier boy an' I said to leave me alone,' he said sourly as the skin split across the man's jawbone. 'Now you ain't goin' to be drinkin' with anyone for a while. Hell, you must be some dumb mule's ass.'

As the man sank to his knees, Edson took a quick glance down at him. Then he picked up his empty glass and walked to the bar.

'Whiskey,' he told the barkeep without a flicker of fuss or mood.

A man in hickory work-clothes drifted up, stood a few paces to the side of Edson. He smiled, said cautiously: 'I'm buyin' that'

Edson exchanged a sharp look with

the barkeep, considered a moment before accepting with a polite nod.

'I guess' you know when you're beat,' the man suggested drolly.

Edson shook his head, spoke quietly. 'Not always. I just don't want to have to do that again.'

'My name's Trimmer Fogg,' the man offered. What you just did . . . you could live off those moments for a hell of a long time.'

'I didn't want a drink. That's all it was,' Edson explained. 'Ain't you got a body to sweep up that rubbish?'

'No. That brat you just smacked? His name's Jimson Bench. He's one o' the curly wolves that move our law on. Our last marshal's workin' his time over in Yellow Dog.' Fogg thought for a moment before continuing. 'That's an interestin' piece you're carryin', son. Whitney, ain't it?'

'Yeah. Had it since I was a kid. Sort o' grown attached to me.'

'Mmmm.' The man eyed Edson carefully 'Once heard of a kid carried that model. Came from south o' town. He put a big .45 into Bur Blackrule's heart. Hit him dead centre.'

For a second, Edson's mind made a turn. 'A .45?' he repeated. 'I heard it was only a .36.' But he hadn't heard any such thing. He was responding with what he knew, what he *thought* he knew.

'Naagh, it was a .45 slug all right. There was an inquest . . . Doc's evidence.' Fogg looked uncertainly at Edson. 'That Whitney. It's a .45 ain't it'?

'The drink don't buy you information, mister. What's your interest in my gun, anyway?' Edson asked cooly.

'I knew some o' Bur Blackrule's punchers. I was in town the night he was murdered. Always reckoned the one who did it would turn up one day.'

'Yeah, they say that happens,' Edson said slow and thoughtful. But his mind was racing. For six years he'd believed it was he who had shot Bur Blackrule. Ever since he'd stood under the lightning, wet and frightened in the mud facing up to Katey Cate.

'If you're sure of what you say, there'll be a record to confirm it . . . the bullet size?' he asked, more drawn in.

'Yeah, at the courthouse. Why *you* so interested in that?'

Edson tried to picture that ill-fated night in his mind. He tried to recall the driving rain and the blackness, his fear. Could it have been someone else who fired the shot that killed Blackrule?

'I'm interested 'cause Whitney revolvers never carried .45 ammo. Whoever it was killed Blackrule, it couldn't o' been that kid from south o' town you mentioned.'

Warily, Fogg eyed Edson. 'That pleases you does it, stranger . . . that news . . . the difference?' he wanted to know.

'I ain't sure 'pleases' is the right word.' Edson drank his whiskey at a gulp. 'Think I'll find myself a hair-cutter,' he said and summarily took his leave.

With barely a glance around him, he walked cheerlessly from the saloon. He stood outside on the narrow boardwalk, felt anger rise to his craw. He thought about renting a horse, swore softly as he looked across the street. For the thousandth time, the old images swam darkly through his mind. He was aiming low, aiming at the ground between Bur Blackrule's feet. Sure he was nervous and shaky, but if he missed, he'd only maim the big wealthy rancher with the whip, not kill him. And now, it sounded like he hadn't. That meant something significant to Edson. It meant that out there some-where was a real killer; a killer who'd shaped the injustice and suffering he'd harboured for all those years.

5

Yellow Dog

Ten miles east of Grey Dog — across
Goose Green — lay its sister town of
Yellow Dog. It was approaching noon
when Edson jogged his grey mare into
Stryders Livery. He clattered over the
boards of a runway into the coolness
of the barn, swung stiffly to the
ground.

He dragged his saddle clear and set it
on a barrel, draped the sweat-soaked
horse blanket across it. He flipped
Stryder a coin.

'Water him an' give him a half-bucket
o' grain,' he said.

A few minutes later, Edson stood
outside the unpainted, boxed structure
of the Digger's Moon. He chewed his
lip reflectively, noted a civic improve-
ment. Out back, a lean-to had been

erected, providing stalls for saddle-brokes. On either side, the town buildings were still strung out in a broken line, their rude appearance disguised by clumps of chaparral. He pushed into the saloon. The place was empty except for three cowboys flipping cards, a snoring drunk and a barkeep who was idly swatting flies.

While his beer was being poured, he read a notice that was hanging prominently before the backbar mirror. He'd done some elementary learning with Ma Gracey, enough to spell out the words. **GUN LAW.** CHECK ALL GUNS AT MY OFFICE — OR SALOON. *Purle Briscoe.* **MARSHAL.**

With six year old warrants probably ageing in all the marshals' offices between Idaho Falls and Boise, Edson wanted no truck with the law. He glanced at the card-players, saw they were all wearing guns. He looked again at the notice, then pushed his Colt across the wet, shiny county.

The barkeep looked puzzled when

Edson nodded at the notice.

'That don't mean nothin',' he said.

'I did wonder. Why don't you take it down?' Edson asked him, taking back the revolver.

The man shrugged. 'Just reminds me of a time I guess, when peace officers enforced their orders.'

'Perle Briscoe,' Edson said. 'I heard o' him. Used to be a good man.'

A few minutes later, Edson headed for the Jasper Hotel. In the dusty lobby, two cowmen were sitting talking. He remembered them straight off. They were from the Cactus T and Howling Wolf spreads. He met their look when he dumped his traps at the desk; he was relieved by the lack of recognition.

Emmett Foyle, who had clerked at the hotel as long as Edson could remember, watched inquisitively as he lettered E. Ringer in the register. Foyle twisted the register around, eyed the name for a moment.

'You rode a ways?' he asked.

Edson shook his head, smiled thinly.

'No. Grey Dog.'

Foyle looked uneasily at the card-players. 'Others have come here lookin' for work. I send 'em across the creek to the Fat B.'

Edson had an immediate dark recollection, his jaw ground at the mention of the Fat B.

'They hirin' guns now?' he asked bitingly.

Once again, Foyle glanced towards the men seated nearby. 'Your room overlooks the street, Mr Ringer. I hope that's OK,' he said courteously, whilst failing to respond to Edson's enquiry.

As Edson climbed the stairs, he wondered. Why, if Foyle thought he was looking for work, didn't the man want advance payment for a room? He shrugged and dumped his traps. Fully dressed, he stretched out on the baggy mattress of the bed, somewhat reassured because no longer was he recognizable as Eddie Riner.

He'd been resting for ten minutes, was drifting off to sleep, when he heard the crack of gunfire from down the street. He groaned and pulled his arms around his ears. 'Goddamn cowpokes,' he moaned and tried again to find some sleep.

It was late in the day when Edson woke. Belly rumblings told him that he needed food and he rolled from the bed. He walked stiffly to the wash-stand, saw the pitcher of water. He dipped in his hand and slicked his hair down, picked up his hat and went back downstairs.

He stood outside the hotel and looked down the street. There was a group of rowdy men standing under the stretched canopy of the Broken Cage saloon. It was of no concern to Edson, so he turned away, crossed the street towards Gries's eating-house.

That was when Purle Briscoe decided to emerge from a side alley. He made his way purposefully towards him.

Edson swore, caught in an immediate rush of panic. The marshal would recognize him, try and shoot him down.

Maybe it had been Stryder or Emmet Foyle after all. Edson resisted an urge to go back as Briscoe came on and closed to less than a dozen paces. He stared into the lawman's face, dared him to recognize him, make a move for his gun. But it had been six years, and Briscoe hardly gave him a glance.

Edson could see the marshal's attention was taken up by the group of men outside the Broken Cage. He guessed it had been them letting off firearms earlier on in the day. Perhaps Purle Briscoe was going to enforce his own order.

With his heart still thumping, he stepped up onto the low plankwalk, then into Gries's. He sat on a wooden stool, took a few deep breaths. The Hollander nodded and carried on looking out the window while Edson squinted at the food list. He'd just decided on meatballs when another gunshot went off down the street. Then there was a second and a third. Johan

Gries growled with aggravation and Edson went for the door.

Men were waving their arms and shouting, running from stores and alleys along the street. Outside the Broken Cage, Purle Briscoe lay flat on his back, motionless in the hard-packed dirt of the street.

By the time Edson reached the nervous townsfolk, they were huddled around the body. He eased his way through, stared down at the dull metal of the marshal's star.

'Anybody see who did this?' he asked of no one in particular.

'I seen 'em.' Milo Treaves, who owned the town's hardware store was at his side. 'Them Fat B gun-hawks,' he said gruffly. 'Old Purle wanted 'em out of town. He said he was goin' to take their guns.'

'He tried to do that . . . on his own?' Edson asked him.

'I reckon he did, yeah. It was Silvy Crawle. There's nothin' so bad, that that man ain't. Old Purle, he's slowed up some, an' I guess the asshole knew that.'

'This man Crawle. You see him go someplace?'

'Back into the Cage.' Treaves took a deep breath. 'With the rest o' Jago Rizzle's dogs.'

'Jago Rizzle?' The interest quickened Edson's voice. He remembered Jago, the son of the Rolling Post owner. 'I knew him once. He's runnin' the Fat B now, is he?'

'Yep, sure is. When his pa died, he married Miss Kate . . . put the Rollin' Post and Fat B together. Now it's the biggest spread in the county.'

Edson's pulse thumped at the mention of Katey, at the thought of Bur Blackrule. 'How come he's hirin' guns?' he asked.

Treaves eyed him warily. 'Are you stringin' me along, mister?'

'Nope. It's of passin' interest . . . no more,' Edson lied. 'I'm a stranger . . . just ridin' through.'

'That'd be for the best, I reckon,'

Treaves said dolefully. 'Blackrule was tough. He pushed us all around, but Jago . . . well he sticks us like pigs. He's out to hogtie the whole o' Snake Plain.'

'Do you think we should telegraph the sheriff . . . get some some deputies sent?' one of the other men asked. 'There ain't no law in Grey Dog, nor here now.'

'Crawle would be into Nevada by the time Cole Morelock got his men here,' Treaves said. 'You bet Jago'd case the knot, even if Crawle got caught,' another voice added.

'That Fat B . . . they roddin' this town from now on,' commented Gries from outside the small group of men. 'They sure scare business away. Then this be some goddammit ghost of a town.'

Treaves agreed, 'Ain't that the truth, Gries. An' lookin' around there's ten, maybe twelve of us here right now, who's goin' to suffer.' The storekeeper continued boldly: 'Let's do somethin' about it. Go get your guns, men

. . . whatever you've got. Bring 'em to the store. This is our town . . . we got to decide who runs it.'

Unease immediately ran around the group, dust rose where feet shuffled. It was plain to see there was no eagerness to meet the Fat B's hired gun-hands. Marshal Purle Briscoe was a grim reminder of the consequences.

Before any of them committed themselves or lost face, Edson's voice held them. 'This don't call for no bog-hole army. I'll get Crawle for you.'

'You arrest him . . . alone?' Gries asked.

Edson smiled. 'Hell, yeah, if it gets me some sleep . . . time to eat some o' your meatballs. But I never said I'd arrest him.'

Milo Treaves kneeled, carefully removed the marshal's badge from Purle Briscoe. He wiped it, looked Edson in the eye as he pinned in to his buck-skin. 'Can't have anyone dispensin' law if they ain't got proper credentials, can we?' he said with a

51

curious glint in his eye. 'You sure we ain't met, stranger? You look kinda familiar.'

'My name's Ringer. I was mistook for Custer not so long ago,' Edson said. 'Perhaps you got that in mind. One o' you good men goin' to watch my back?' he then asked calmly.

A man stepped forward. He was younger than the others. 'You got him,' he said with what sounded like enthusiasm.

'What's your name?' Edson asked.

'Parker Buck . . . saddlebum,' came the reply.

'Good enough for this town,' Edson muttered. 'Let's go bag us a turkey.'

A pall of anxiety fell across the group of mostly small-time business men as they withdrew. They watched tense and uncertain as Buck and Edson turned on the Broken Cage.

Then another man emerged from the saloon. He stepped down into the street, away from the stretched awning. He was tall and lean, had bleak expressionless eyes. Silvy Crawle stood determinedly with his legs slightly apart. His stance was that of a confident gunman and his left hand hovered close to the butt of a tied-down revolver.

Edson made up his mind. He moved fast, didn't hesitate as he approached Crawle. It made the gunman uncertain; he expected Edson to slow, falter as he got near. He moved fractionally, the heel of his hand touching the butt of his gun.

'You'll be Crawle, the killer?' Edson called.

'Who the hell are you? Get back!' spat back the gunman, in unforeseen panic.

Edson saw the fingers of Crawle's left hand twitch but he didn't slow. He carried on, his aggressive force transferring itself to his own gun-hand.

Crawle was panicked at Edson's nerve, pulled his gun when there was less than six paces between them. But the confrontation was of Edson's making, and he'd always had the advantage.

'You ain't supposed to . . . Crawle had started to say as he fired, when Edson's .36-calibre bullet hit him. His own bullet whined past Edson's ear, and he fired again as his legs buckled. He staggered one step forward, then hit the ground. He pushed up his long frame, made every effort to level his gun-hand. 'Goddamn pilgrim. You ain't supposed to do that,' he exhaled. Then he crumpled, spat into the ground and lay very still.

'An' you ain't supposed to shoot down old men in the street, you son of a bitch,' Edson shouted into the dusk. He took a few steps forward and with the toe of his boot, lift-kicked Crawle's gun into the middle of the street. Then he turned to the men who now stood craven and quiet, watching from the doorway of the Broken Cage. 'Check in your guns!' he snarled at them.

6

A Clean Sweep

Edson heard spur chains tremble as someone else came out, stepped down from the Broken Cage. The man didn't look at Edson or the bodies of Crawle or Briscoe. He simply brushed past, peevishly sauntered off down the street. The rest of the Fat B men turned away, slunk back into the gloom of the cowman's bar.

Through the door, Edson moved to one side and stood with his back to the wall, watched as two of the men placed their guns on the bar. Then he glanced around the murky, foul-smelling room. Two more men were making a pretence of conversation as he stepped up close behind them.

He drove his knuckles in hard against the bigger man's kidneys, took a step back as the man half-stumbled against the bar.

'I said to check your guns,' he snapped as the man gasped with pain.

Both men pulled their Colts. The one who'd been hit looked spitefully at Edson.

'I'll remember your face mister. You won't always be wearin' that badge.'

Edson appeared not to hear, turned away unconcerned. A Fat B gunhand who'd been watching Edson closely, laughed out loud.

'Hey Marshal, you stayin' for a drink? You surely deserve one. There ain't many would go up against six fearsome gunnies.'

Edson grinned. 'I only thought of it as one at a time,' he said. 'An' I wasn't on my own.' He knew the type of men he was dealing with. They were unimaginative and had no respect for life; theirs or anyone else's. They were mercenary killers. 'I'll stay for a peaceful drink,' he informed the man. 'An' if anyone so much as coughs . . . I swear I'll blow their head away.'

Men from the street and Digger's Moon were drifting in now. They were curious to see how Edson had fared, to rub shoulders with the newly appointed lawman.

Gries's big shoulders were heaving as he ordered up glasses of beer. 'You done much marshallin'?' he chortled. 'You got good style. You won't live long . . . but you got good style.'

Edson took a long draught from his beer, winked at Parker Buck as he approached. Then he put down his glass and frowned meaningfully at the carbine Buck was proudly carrying.

'What! You want *me* to hand in *my* gun?' The young man read Edson's look.

Edson nodded. 'Yeah. Nobody's deputized you yet.'

'I know . . . but, Jeez.' Slightly miffed, Buck laid his gun across the bar top, lowered his voice. 'I thought you'd want to know, Marshal. There's some moody *hombre* outside, an' I reckon he's waitin' for you. Want me to look to your back again?'

Edson drained the last of his beer. 'Thanks,' he said, 'but no. I know who it is.

'You know . . . ?' Buck was echoing as Edson pushed away from the bar.

The town was goin' into full dark. Crawle's body was merging with the dust, but Edson could see that Purle Briscoe had already been taken from the street. The peevish gunny who'd walked away from the saloon was sitting on the plankwalk, his back against an upright. He grunted, spat into the dust when Edson appeared. 'I come back,' he said.

'I knew you would. I guess you're just tired o' livin',' Edson countered wearily.

The man swore and fell sideways, dashed a hand for his gun. But Edson was on him. He lashed out a foot, caught the man in his backside. Then he stepped quickly around him, booted hard in the back of his neck.

'You worthless runt,' he grated.

The man made a choking sound in his throat, tried to twist his body to gain a shot upwards.

Edson pulled his Colt and stooped, brought the barrel down hard across the man's bony forearm. He winced at the crack, felt the blow run to his shoulder.

'I'll take your gun . . . put it somewhere safe,' he told the man who was racked with pain.

As he stepped to the ground, a shrill voice cut the darkness.

'What are you doing? What have you done to that man?'

Edson froze, turned his head slowly. Coming towards him, her face pale and colourless in the dark was a girl in a tight wrap-around coat.

'What are you doing, kicking him? Is he drunk?' she asked brusquely.

Edson shook his head vigorously. 'No ma'am. He was about to shoot me.'

'We'll he's in no condition to shoot you now,' the girl said.

Edson stooped to retrieve the man's

gun. He snatched it, tossed it into the Broken Cage's water trough.

'First thing in the morning, I'm telling the marshal about this,' she snapped angrily.

'Ahh, that'll be me, ma'am. Briscoe's dead. Got himself shot, not more'n ten minutes ago.'

The young lady's mouth opened and closed. She caught sight of the badge attached to Edson's vest. 'You. You're the one who . . . ' she started to say.

'Yes, ma'am. But from now on, if it enables me to get a meal and a few hours' uninterrupted sleep, I'll be whoever you or anybody else wants. I'm a marshal who's gettin' too tired to argue,' Edson told her.

She thought for a moment, then sniffed. 'Hateful town,' she said, then flounced back across the street.

* * *

It was full dark, but not late, and Edson could see the hardware store was lit up and still open. The bell pinged once as he opened the door and he looked around, wondering if there was any ammunition for his Whitney Colt. He saw Milo Treaves sitting at a desk in a small back office and the man waved him in.

'I had to get back. Business neglected is business lost.' Treaves stretched out a hand to push papers off the seat of a chair, motioned for Edson to sit. 'Yellow Dog is in your debt, Mr Ringer. What you accomplished here this evening was very impressive,' he said thoughtfully.

'It might have looked that way, but I still ain't eaten,' Edson replied.

Treaves laid down a pen, placed the fingertips of both hands together. He considered a moment before speaking.

'We'll make sure you get watered and fed . . . never fear. I've been considering something else, Mr Ringer. Something for you to consider while Johan Gries is cooking up his finest meatballs.'

'An' what would that be?'

'Staying in the country for a while. A man with your talents could benefit,' Treaves suggested.

I'd o' said the opposite, Edson immediately thought to himself. 'An' just what benefits would they be in Yellow Dog?' he asked instead.

'A hundred . . . maybe hundred an' fifty dollars a month. A nice hotel room. A shiny badge, an' all the ammunition you can use,' Treaves answered, as if he'd had the answer ready.

'You got the authority to offer all that?'

'There's enough of us to see it gets done, Mr Ringer.'

Edson raised an eyebrow. 'You talkin' of here, or Grey Dog?'

'Right here. But our council *does* have central administration for both towns.'

The irony of being offered a peace-keeper's job wasn't lost on Edson.

'I'd never considered such a thing,' he said, which was a dyed-in-the-wool truth. 'What happened to Briscoe over in Grey Dog?' he asked, trying to sound only half-interested, innocent.

'He was run out o' town. One of Jago Rizzle's men ridiculed him, put on pressure . . . same as he did to a few others over the years.'

'Yeah, I heard somethin' to the effect when I rode through there,' Edson said, bending the truth. But he was suddenly thinking of things that were yet to be; like finding the truth of Bur Blackrule's killing through the authority of a marshal's badge.

'A hundred fifty a month is a lot more than I'd make punchin' cows.' Edson closed his eyes in thought for a moment. 'Town marshals are deputized by the county sheriff, aren't they?' he asked.

'That's right. Cole Morelock,' Treaves agreed.

'How much will he want to know about me? I ain't exactly arrived in town preachin' the good book.'

Treaves worked up an indulgent

smile. 'You leave that to me . . . us. Morelock's a reasonable man . . . understands our particular problem.'

It was Edson's turn to understand. 'Yeah, I just bet he does,' he said. But he was uncertain, didn't want an inquisitive lawman asking questions. Not if he had another plan.

Treaves could see the hesitation. 'We need a strong man to reinforce the law,' he encouraged, 'not a preacher. I . . . we believe you're that man, Edson . . . if I may.' He picked a bunch of keys off his desk, held them up. 'These go with the badge,' he said.

'I never had much schoolin' to speak of . . . book-learning'.'

Treaves considered what Edson was saying. 'I see. Well yes, there are records to keep. Mostly for the county auditor. Daily schedules, rosters, pay-outs and the like. But as I said, we are the administrators . . . that means we can handle any bookkeeping. What do you say now?' he asked.

Edson took the keys. 'I'm thinkin','

he said in slow response, 'that right now, there's almost certainly worse things in life.'

Treaves looked relieved. 'Good, good man. There's one thing though,' he added tentatively. 'The gun law, of old Purle's. I approve of it of course . . . most of the town do, but it hasn't been enforced for a long while now.'

Edson looked quizzical. 'And you want it to be?'

'Yes, yes of course, but . . . well you see, there's a big trail herd, and it's already well north o' Brigham City. That means the punchers will be riding into town . . . probably tonight. The boys will be wild, but they're different stock from Jago's gunhands. There's no need to tell you Yellow Dog welcomes their hard-earned dollars. So a little leniency . . . tolerance please, Marshal. You do understand?'

'Yeah, tolerance. I know the word. It's what most nesters are towards the likes o' Rizzle and other *rico* ranchers. I'll tolerate 'em, if that's what you want.

In fact, how's about I check with you every mornin'? Find out who to kill . . . who not to.'

'You sound bitter, Edson. This isn't a personal thing, is it? It's all part of bending with the law, you know.'

'Yeah I guess it is. I got a lot to learn,' Edson said. But he remembered how a lot of folk felt about the likes of Ma Gracey and her waifs and strays; how Bur Blackrule felt about young Eddie Riner. And that had very little to do with tolerance or bending the law.

The distant Raft River mountains were etched black and sharp against the indigo sky when Edson left the store. He brought to mind the cabin in the timberline, Ma Gracey and little Birdy, the wood-framed mirror and Katey Cate. Then he shivered at the approaching chill, badly wanted his meal and hoped Gries was up for serving him.

The Hollander was waiting. He said the bowl of steaming meatballs and side plate of fried potatoes were on the house.

Thirty minutes later, Edson was wiping his lips when a weary-looking townsman entered the small eating-place. The man dropped a black Gladstone on the greasy floor.

'John, you bring in that firewater you're suckin' on,' he called out to Gries.

The doctor didn't say anything more until he got the bottle of schnapps in front of him. Gries handed him a small glass, watched as Pounce filled it.

Pounce eyed his drink, winked at Edson. 'I'm Dorset Pounce. Genuine Jimmy, Old Pills, Sawbones, even Town Doctor. Call me what you like. And by the look o' that badge, you'll be Yellow Dog's newly appointed marshal,' he said affably. The doctor grunted gently as the schnapps went down. Then he moved his stool back. 'They keep you busy on Snake Plain. Ain't slept for six months.'

Edson smiled. 'That's busy,' he agreed.

'You know, there are three chapters

in the story of a cow town, Marshal. In the beginning it's new-found and wild. Then it gets tamed and reformation starts.'

'Who by?'

'Settlers. The Law. Women. Preachers.'

'You said *three* chapters.'

'That's when everybody leaves . . . the town dies. Right now both Grey and Yellow Dog are in the early grip of reform.' The doctor smiled and took another mouthful of schnapps.

'Thanks for lettin' me sit in on class,' Edson said, pleasantly. He thought sometime he'd get to know Pounce better, get to like him even. 'Now I think I'll take a walk along the street. Start some o' that reformin' maybe,' he said and bid goodnight.

Half a day earlier, he'd ridden into Yellow Dog guarded, uneasy of the law. Now he wore a marshal's badge and had the backing of the town's leading businessmen. But how did Treaves and his cohorts expect him to close herd a pack of punchers when the juice got to them. A good time, beating up a storm, firing guns was all they wanted. In Edson's own interest, he'd somehow have to enforce Purle Briscoe's order. There was only four, maybe five more hours to daybreak. But for a cow-puncher on a bender, that was a dangerously long time.

From down the street, a woman's squeal broke through the roistering of the Broken Cage. For a moment he wondered if it was the irate girl who'd upbraided him earlier. He doubted it, chortled quietly at the thought.

7

First Shots

Marshal Edson Ringer tugged at the wide brim of his hat and headed straight for the clamour. If he couldn't enforce a gun law, there was no point to what he was doing, he'd already decided. He might just as well ride on. 'No killing,' Milo Treaves had said, protected by his money and merchandise. Well, hell, Edson thought. Fate had returned him, now there was a price to pay for his six wilderness years. Time wasn't always the healer. Maybe a few bystanders, innocents, would suffer, if they got in the way.

He faltered, wondered about the sound of a gunshot from back along the street. He took a deep breath and stepped into the cloying discord of the saloon. In tobacco smoke so thick it misted the hanging oil-lamps, it was obvious that punchers heading for the Bozeman trail had arrived. There was only one problem from Edson's standpoint; almost every man was armed. He knew that in an hour or two, when the beer and red-eye took control of brains and tempers, the guns would speak.

Shoving his way across the room, he moved for the bleary-eyed piano player. When Edson's hand gripped his shoulder, the man turned his head. He focused on the marshal's badge, and his bony hands slid from the keyboard.

'Y'all remove your guns,' Edson yelled when the music stopped. 'Lay 'em on the bar. Pick 'em up when you leave town,' he ordered, less confident.

As he expected, no one moved. He read the astonishment, then the hostility in their eyes. A cowpoke just drunk enough to be dangerous lumbered towards him.

'I don't give up my gun for nobody,' the man sneered.

'I'm the marshal of Yellow Dog

. . . not a nobody,' Edson retorted 'If you won't put up your gun, leave town . . . if you can still ride.'

The man staggered to one side as a leg gave way and he clawed at his gun. But Edson hit him. He punched him hard and low in the gut, knowing the man would go down, cause no more trouble.

Edson felt the sting of resentment around him, wondered when the next man would retaliate.

'I'll shoot the next man who feels the same way,' he said, knowing he'd lit a short fuse. He was brushing his long buckskin coat to one side, when suddenly one of three or four saloon girls hoisted herself onto the bar.

'Stop,' she cried out. 'Most o' you bull brains forgot what the law is around here, but we still got it. It's just newly packaged,' she said, casting a bright eye at Edson.

There were a few catcalls and bawdy whistles.

'You tell 'em, Sweet Dove,' a voice

roared. Edson, tense with strain, stared at the girl.

'Which o' you galoots needs to pack a rod?' she said. 'Next to the law, I'm the only danger you'll find in the Broken Cage. If I'm checkin' in my little shooter, you can too. What do you say?'

Amid more lascivious whooping, the girl stood down, deftly extricated a derringer from a leg garter. It broke the lethal confrontation and men laughed, started to stack their belts and guns under the back bar mirror.

Edson propped himself against a side wall, nodded for the man to start playing the piano again. He took off his hat and drew a finger around the damp inner band, pushed it back on his head when he saw the saloon boss approach.

'Seems like you're hell bent on closin' us down, Marshal,' Slick Midland proposed. 'You're either very very good with that pistol or you're a chancer.'

'You're a gambler. What do you

reckon, Mr. Midland?'

Midland pulled a slim cigar from his top pocket. 'I reckon, if it weren't for our little Dove, someone would o' been scrapin' you off the floor right about now.'

Edson nodded stoically 'Yeah, maybe,' he said. 'Either way, I meant what I said. An' that includes the vest pistol you're carryin' under your coat. You hear me good, Midland. If I find any one else in this dump packin' iron, I'll close it up with you still inside.'

Edson pushed past Midland. On instinct, he turned to see Dove was standing at the bar watching him. He thought he saw, sensed something other than an encounter of eyes. But he just touched the brim of his hat, said 'thank you,' as he left the saloon.

Outside, the night breezes chilled his nervous sweat. He was weary to his bones, thought of his hotel bed. As long as the punchers were in town there'd be no peace until daybreak. Suddenly events didn't seem to be entirely within his control.

He looked into the dark interiors of stores, walked briskly past grim alleyways. He left the plankwalks and stepped across the street. Compared to the Broken Cage, Diggers' Moon was a haven of rest. And so it should be at three o'clock in the morning, he thought.

He strolled to the marshal's office, a narrow clay-brick and clapboard building annexed to the town's grain store. He pulled his keys, then noticed a deep shadow from the partly open door. He cautiously stepped inside, fumbled at a still warm lamp that was hanging from the ceiling.

The old swamper from Diggers' Moon whom Treaves had arranged to clean up the office was slumped in the marshal's chair. 'Drunk as a skunk,' Edson thought aloud as he shook the man's shoulder. But as the lamplight grew, he saw the dark spread of blood. He raised the grizzled head, looked into dull, unseeing eyes.

'Goddammit,' Edson yelled, his stomach churning. 'That gunshot.' He gripped the man under his arms and dragged him from the chair, laid him under the lamp. He saw the lean features, distressed skin jacket, long grey hair and it all came clear. In the weak light, probably from across the street, the old swamper had been mistaken for Edson Ringer the new marshal. He'd been shot through the part-open doorway. Edson swore, swore again. It didn't add up. Who in hell's name would shoot the new marshal?

He pinched out the lamp-wick. In bleak, confused mood, he turned the key of his office. He looked up and down the street, recalled a conversation he'd had in Grey Dog about the bullet-size of a Whitney Colt; the conversation when he'd realized that someone else was guilty of the murder of Bur Blackrule. Maybe that was the real killer out there, scared and panicked that after six years, a grown-up Eddie Riner was back in the dog towns for retribution.

Edson had another tough bout of cursing. He knew that when the marksman learned of his mistake, he'd have to try again. If that was the set-up in Yellow Dog, Edson was up to his neck in trouble. So now he was angry. He wanted to give someone else the chance of a crack at him, and there was no place more suited than the Broken Cage.

The swing-door of the saloon lashed back when he went in. The men who were still drinking saw the challenge in his eyes as he bulled towards the bar. The barkeep who was mopping the top of the bar looked up, nodded nervously.

'What's your name, feller?' Edson asked him.

'Loomis,' said the man sourly. 'Call me Ticker.'

'Well, Loomis, the next time I see somethin' in this goddamn bar I don't like, you get pasted. Understand?'

'Why? Why you turnin' on me? I

don't carry a gun.'

'Because I don't like this place, an' I probably don't like you, Loomis. Now get yourself out from behind there an' find Midland. You tell him I want to see him. Tell him to come find me . . . wherever I am.'

Loomis wasn't going to argue. He dropped his sopping cloth, edged uneasily to the side door.

Edson stepped in close. 'Tell him if he don't come, I'll burn the place down,' he said. Then he backed off, but once again he experienced a curious gut feeling. Dove turned to face him. Her face was full of sadness and she smiled weakly, found difficulty with her words.

'Don't you recognize me? It is you . . . isn't it . . . Eddie?' she asked.

Edson gulped, stared full into the girl's dark gleaming eyes. 'Reckon you got me tagged wrong, ma'am. You're close, but the name's . . . Edson. Edson Ringer,' he corrected.

Dove bit her lip, shook her head imperceptively.

Edson raised his hand, ran his fingertips across a small gash that scarred one of his cheekbones.

Dove's teeth gleamed in a quick smile. 'That's a *tag* I ain't ever likely to get wrong,' she teased.

'Birdy?' Edson uttered as recognition dawned. He could only stare, Little Birdy. The kid who'd sat on her cot in Ma Gracey's cabin, sewing . . . on silk purses. Could six years and the Broken Cage have done this to her, grown her up so much?

'If it's Slick you're waitin' for, why not stay. Sit here with me . . . please?' Dove asked considerately. Before Edson had time to consider she'd grabbed a bottle of whiskey from behind the bar.

'What you doin' here Birdy?' Edson asked as he sat down. 'This ain't a fittin' place. What happened? Where's Ma?'

'Ma? After you left us, we went back into the Rafters. Went so far back we made it to Salt Lake City. That's where they got some holy rollers, Eddie, an'

79

that weren't for me. I left it a couple o' years, then come back. Not as Little Birdy, though.' Dove poured two full glasses. 'Seems like you did the same . . . come back as someone else.'

'You forgot there was half o' Snake River lookin' to stretch my neck, Birdy? Could be some of 'em still are.'

'I ain't forgot, Eddie. But that was some years ago. You've changed . . . grown up some.'

Edson downed his whiskey. 'That's right, so less of the Eddie. It's Edson now,' he told her. He remembered the times when candles had been pinched out and he'd confided his thoughts to Little Birdy. 'There's a dead man, Birdy,' he said without preamble. 'He's stretched out in the marshal's office. He's been shot by someone thinkin' it was me. I know it.'

'That'll be the scum that sticks to Silvy Crawle. You made a bad impression on them, Ed . . . Edson.'

'No, not them, Birdy. There's someone else wants me dead, an' it ain't nothin' to do with Crawle, or Marshal Ringer.'

'Oh I reckon it is, Eddie. But don't ask me why, 'cause right now I can't tell you.' Birdy filled Edson's glass, told him it was on the house when he raised an eyebrow. 'Why don't you leave Yellow Dog, Eddie?' she asked him. 'There's nowhere to go with Jago Rizzle. Go back to where it was you come from.'

'I was aimin' to, Birdy, but I got held up . . . so to speak. But somethin' happened over in Grey Dog an' now I ain't goin' anywhere. Not till I've run down Bur Blackule's killer.' Immediately, Edson looked hard for Birdy's surprise, the challenge.

The long night's gettin' to you Eddie. In case you forgot, it was *you* shot Blackrule. That's why you been gone for six years.'

Edson took his second whiskey. 'No Birdy, it weren't me. The bullet that hit Blackrule was a .45. My Whitney carries .36s, an' that's a fact.'

'You can prove that, Eddie?' Birdy was excited and eager. 'Who would it've been?'

'East or west o' Goose Creek, Birdy, you name 'em. But whoever it was, was here in town tonight.'

Birdy was quiet, deeply troubled. 'I'll . . . ' she started to say.

Edson had caught sight of Loomis skulking back into the saloon. 'You'll stay here until it's time to leave. Start thinkin' about what you're goin' to do after,' he told her affectionately.

'What about you? Where are you goin' now, Eddie?' Birdy wanted to know.

'I got to tell someone they're a potman short,' Edson said angrily.

Edson made his way towards the solitary flare that was guttering outside Diggers' Moon. He was within sixty feet when the crash and flame of a gunshot stabbed out from the blackness of a nearby alleyway. He sensed the pulse of air as the bullet grazed the nape of his neck. He whirled with the explosion in his head. He hurled himself forward into the ground, pulled frantically at his Colt as a window shattered across the street. The landing jarred him, took his breath away. But he held his arms firm, triggered off two shots into the night.

Cowpunchers stumbled from the saloons, stood drunk and hesitant as they sought out the gunfire.

Edson got to his feet, half-bent, and ran at the alley. He pitched himself into the gloom, edged his way fast along the clapboarding. Trash littered the narrow space. Broken, empty crates were stacked high, and he kicked out at cans and bottles. He stood motionless, listening, but nothing moved. There was no sound other than his own heavy breathing, scuttling rodents. The gunman was either lying for him in the deep dark, or had returned to nearby shelter.

Edson blew hard, then took a few deep breaths before turning back to the main street. Birdy was among the group of men who stood beneath the stretched canopy of the Broken Cage.

'What's happened? You been shot at, Marshal?' Birdy cried out. She was concerned, tried to avoid any discernible familiarity that others might pick up on.

Edson could see her eyes glistening. 'Yeah . . . again,' he breathed heavily as he brushed past her, back into the saloon.

Loomis was there, but didn't have time to take evasive action before Edson was on him.

'You've never been so close to dyin', mister,' he rasped at the barkeep. 'Now, answer real careful. Did you give my message to Midland?'

Loomis's eyes stared, his jaw dropped.

'The boss is asleep. He'd fire me for disturbin' him.'

'An' that worries you? Have you any idea what it's like tryin' to wash glasses with ten broken fingers, you imbecile?' Edson swore at him. 'No, he ain't asleep,' he said more calmly. 'He's wide awake, starin' at the ceilin' . . . wonderin' if his luck's just run out.'

With that Edson swung away and went for the door, didn't slow until he reached Jasper's Hotel. He dragged his legs up the creaky stairs, his body racked with tiredness and despair. He could see his bed outlined by the first streaks of daybreak, realized he hadn't got to Diggers' Moon. Then he worried about Birdy, what she was doing as Dove. As he fell asleep he reckoned that as far as the dog towns were concerned, there wasn't much difference from coming from nowhere to being somewhere.

8

The Odds Lengthen

Later the same morning most of Yellow Dog was indolently preparing for the new day when Edson pulled a handcart to the edge of town. Storekeepers who'd been sweeping their plankwalks sneaked covert looks when they saw the body. It was the luckless old swamper who'd stopped the bullet intended for Marshal Ringer.

Sitting on a bench, boot-heels up on the handrail, Parker Buck was dozing out front of the Diggers' Moon saloon. But when Edson returned, the 'saddlebum' had moved; was now in the marshal's office, sitting behind the untidy desk.

Edson's eyes narrowed. 'The last person to sit in that chair's sniffin' wood,' he said. 'Some gunsman mistook him for me.'

'Jeez!' Buck exclaimed, getting up quick. 'An' someone took a shot at you last night, I'm hearin'. You better take care if it happens a third time, Marshal.'

'I thought that was for *good* luck?' Edson said, dropping into his chair. 'But then most *hombres* who pin on a star die with their boots on.'

Buck nodded as if in agreement. 'There's four graves bein' dug out o' town. Fellers in the Birdcage say one of 'em's for you. They're offerin' ten to one you'll be joinin' Crawle and Briscoe before the month's out.'

Barely amused, Edson raised an eyebrow, 'Hmmm, ten to one . . . that sounds like a compliment. But just for today, I'll steer clear o' boot hill.'

'Yep. If I was you, I'd do the same. Me? I got a trip planned along Snake River doin' some trail findin'. Should be back in a day or two though. You take care o' yourself, you hear,

Marshal. You ain't got me watchin' your back.'

★　★　★

Mid morning, Edson was hogging a strip of shade as he strolled the plankwalk. He carried his Colt tucked into the waistband of his pants. To Edson's mind it was less intimidating, though it gave little clue to his own unease. But he did notice that although no one was openly packing a gun, the people too, appeared nervous, wary of trouble.

He hesitated outside Milo Treaves's hardware store, watched as three riders trotted their horses into the south end of town. Their leader was mounted on a fine-looking blood bay, but it was the rider that most interested Edson.

The man from the combined Rolling Post and Fat B ranches had grown some. Edson noted the trappings of wealth: the fine clothes, ornately tooled saddle, handsome Colt. But other than that, and unlike Edson, Jago Rizzle hadn't changed that much.

The two riders trailing him were saddle-worn, but they were alert, had a certain foxiness that warned of their work. One, Edson recognized as Denver John. He was the gun hand from the Broken Cage, who'd offered to buy him a drink after he'd shot Silvy Crawle.

So the cock-a-doodle-doo of Snake Plain had come to town, had he? Edson thought. He watched carefully, considered the situation.

Rizzle pulled up outside the Broken Cage where he swung to the ground and loose-hitched his mount. His two henchmen remained in their saddles, their hands folded on the butts of their guns. Rizzle stepped onto the plankwalk under the awning, looked warily up and down the street.

And then Edson realized what the town was waiting for. Jago Rizzle had ridden in for a face-off with the newly appointed marshal.

As was his style, Edson moved quick

and purposeful. He made straight for the three men, conscious of the many eyes that would be following him. Rizzle was looking in the other direction, but Denver John saw him advancing and muttered a warning.

'You're inside town limits, friends. Check those Colts, like the order says.' It was forceful advice, but given with no obvious threat. It was, more or less, the only thing that Edson wanted to say.

A little surprised, Rizzle turned quickly to face Edson. He curled his lip at the star pinned to the faded buckskin.

'So you're the scoop they made marshal?' he said insolently.

Edson seemed unperturbed. 'Just do as the law demands, an' check in your guns,' he repeated.

The rancher bristled. 'He don't know who I am, John. You tell him.'

Denver John grinned, fascinated by the confrontation. 'You ain't supposed to go makin' demands of Jago Rizzle, Marshal. Reckon it's *his* laws people listen to around here.'

Edson's voice hardened. 'It ain't personal, Rizzle, so don't make it so. Remove your jewellery or leave town. Them's your choices.'

'Don't you give me choices, Ringer. A nod from me an' you're dead meat.' Rizzle's voice was hoarse, suppressed rage showed in his eyes, the gnash of his jaw.

The marshal stepped closer. 'Oh, I'll die all right,' he threatened. 'But you won't be alive to see it.'

Rizzle was about to hit back, realized he'd lost. 'I ain't leavin' town,' he said, holding up his hands in mock submission. 'I'll put my gun where I can see it.' With that, he pushed into the bar. The few customers watched in imminent fear as the powerful ranch-owner stepped up to the bar, slung his gun and belt across the counter.

'And the hideaway,' Edson prompted from the doorway.

Rizzle jerked out a small-calibre pistol, pushed it after his Colt.

'Give him the drink he came into town for,' the marshal nodded, glaring at Loomis. 'Mr Rizzle looks like he needs coolin' down.'

Loomis understood the threat in Edson's voice. He slammed a full bottle of whiskey onto the bar and watched helplessly as the marshal backed away through the door.

Denver John and his accomplice moved aside from where they'd been watching the play.

'You too. An' I ain't got time to pass the time o' day,' Edson told them plainly.

'Perhaps next time we'll just shoot.' Denver John's pale eyes locked with the marshal's as the two men edged past him into the bar.

'I'll bear it in mind,' Edson murmured. He watched, waited as the two gunmen placed their guns alongside Rizzle's.

The rancher shouted a threat, his voice shaking with anger, but Edson had gone.

★ ★ ★

That same evening, Slick Midland was offering twenty to one that Yellow Dog's marshal would take the open grave in Boot Hill before a week had passed. There were few takers.

In the marshal's office Edson sat pondering his luck. He made himself some strong coffee, recalled his few years in the timberline with Little Birdy and Ma Gracey. The humiliation of being an orphan and poor had lanced deep, as did his feelings for those that provoked it. Even now, memories of the Rolling Post made his hackles rise. Old Mose Rizzle, who'd owned the spread, always had a kindly nod, even pennies for a fancy doodad. But Jago, the spoiled son, had taken malicious delight in tormenting him whenever he'd come to their yard. Jago was two or three years older than Edson and he'd had a saddle pony, a squirrel gun and schooling. Now, apparently, he'd got Katey Cate as his wife.

To stop losing himself in reflection Edson decided he'd go for a stroll; make the rounds before full dark. Outside the hardware store he noticed a horse that was shod for riding rough country. He waited five minutes until its owner stepped from Treaves's store. He decided he didn't know the man who carried a gun holstered high around his waist.

The man glanced in his direction. 'I'm leaving town, Marshal. Can't see any reason to stay . . . certainly nothin' worth shootin' at,' he said openly.

Edson nodded. 'Let's hope you're right, cowboy,' he returned with genuine frankness.

The man mounted his horse and Edson went into the store to see Milo Treaves.

Treaves didn't seem overly pleased to see him, but obviously had something on his mind.

'You're pushin' Slick Midland, Marshal. I thought we agreed you'd go easy on the law an' order,' he started off.

'I never agreed to nothin'.'

'For God's sake,' Treaves flared, 'you practically challenged him to a gun-fight.'

Edson immediately wondered how he knew that. 'We can't have lawless quarters,' he said. 'Not if this town's gettin' to the second chapter I've heard so much about.'

'Yeah, well maybe you're too handy with your gun . . . maybe we all got it wrong. Do you have any idea what trouble you're bringin' down on the town by what you did to Jago Rizzle?'

'I got the best part of a month to serve out, Mr Treaves, before I quit.'

Treaves looked around him uncertainly. 'Stay away from the Broken Cage then. Do your work elsewhere.'

'That bucket o' blood's where I earn my best money. What's it matter to you anyways?'

'I own it, for Chrissakes.'

Edson stared hard as it came clear. 'Of course you do. That an' half the rest of the town, I'll bet. Well I'm sorry, but as long as I'm wearin' this star, I'll at least try an' honour it. I was taught how to do that, if not much else.'

Treaves considered the problem for a moment. 'I could make that month's pay, five hundred dollars. Edson. Think about it,' he advised.

'I already have. I told you. It's to do with keepin' my word.'

'Yeah, right. Have it your own way. Let's hope you at least live to regret it. Now if you'll excuse me, Marshal, I've other business to attend to.'

Five minutes later Edson was back in his office, sipping more coffee. He sat back, considering his troubles as he went through a sheaf of dog-eared wanted posters. He was 'making more enemies than you could shake a stick at', was how Ma Gracey would have put it. It was getting late now, and he knew the peril darkness would bring; as it already had for the old swamper. Common sense told him to get out before they tipped him into the hole that Parker Buck told him about. In fact, he could team up with the 'saddlebum' in whatever he was doing along the Snake River. No, damn 'em all, he thought. He'd leave town of his own accord, not theirs.

'And what would you be muttering about marshal?' Edson heard her voice, blinked himself back to full alert. Her name was Estrella Mace and she stood in the office doorway, as formal and abrupt as the last time they'd met.

'Guess I was dreamin' ma'am.'

'I can imagine,' she said. 'You must have plenty on your conscience.' She glanced around distastefully. 'Has no one ever cleaned this place?'

'It don't bother me. There was someone, but he . . . ' Edson faltered, wasn't prepared to finish his explanation.

'Yes, I'm sorry, Milo Treaves said you had some auditing that needs doing. Perhaps I could help? My name's Estrella Mace.'

'Yes, ma'am. And there sure is bits an' pieces, you could help with. I'll look 'em out for you some time. I ain't had time to get around to that part o' the job yet. I been sort o' busy.'

Estrella Mace looked suddenly discomfited. 'That time I saw you . . . in the street. Well I may have been mistaken.'

'Yes ma'am, you were. That's the sort o' work I'm paid for.'

Estrella Mace gave a stiff, distant smile, 'If you can sort out those papers for me, I'll stop by,' she said. 'Good night, Marshal Ringer.'

'Good night, ma'am . . . Miss Mace . . . Estrella, and thank you.'

It was full dark when Edson returned from his meal at Johan Gries's. The trail crews had lit out for the home ranches and very little stirred, even in and around the Broken Cage. Nevertheless, before he lit the hanging lamp, he jammed his slicker across the one window that fronted the street. Trouble was clawing at him, and he wasn't going to give the old swamper's killer a chance for a second shot.

He sat for many minutes drumming his fingers on the edge of his desk, going through some muddled thinking, waiting.

'Marshal? Marshal Ringer? You in there? Mr Midland says to get you. Some drunk's threatenin' to shoot up the Broken Cage,' Loomis called through the door.

Edson actioned his Colt, placed it on the desk in front of him.

'You get back, Loomis. Tell Midland, I'll be there,' he answered back. So that was the pathetic, wretched plan, Edson thought. He was supposed to believe that a professional gambler couldn't take care of a roostered cowpoke. Well, thanks to Loomis, he know knew what was coming, what they had in store for him — a bullet as soon as he pushed through the swing doors. Blame it on the cowpoke.

Edson eased open the door to the street, and by the faint light that entered, pulled a sawed-off shotgun from a wall shelf. It was a weapon that had seen a life, but it was an effective law-officer's gun when loaded with buckshot. He could see it had rarely been cleaned or oiled in years, allowed himself a justifiable string of curses. He wrenched up the twin barrels, and kicked the door shut as he stepped onto the plankwalk.

9

Gunmen Of Broken Cage

At a run, the shotgun tucked underneath his left arm, Edson slanted across the street. He turned sharply to avoid a brea flare outside the Broken Cage. There were three horses tied to the rail where an hour ago there'd been a dozen. There was no piano music and the interior of the saloon was gloomy and unwelcoming. He made for the narrow alley with its rats and rubbish. Breathing hard, he stopped before a closed door at the side-rear of the building. Gripping the shotgun, he tentatively turned the knob. The door eased against its hinges, and he stepped inside. Around him, in the low light that filtered through a glazed door, he could see the trappings of a sparsely furnished room. It was Slick Midland's bolthole, and from the coloured-glass panel on the door, Edson knew it connected to the back bar of the saloon.

He took a couple of deep breaths, knew that Ma Gracey would have recommended a few '*Praise the Lords*'. Then he opened the door and stepped quickly through, looked across the almost empty room.

For a long, curious moment no one noticed him. Three men were intent on watching the front door and Midland was sitting against a side wall. Then a startled cry from Loomis, who stood at the far end of the bar, split the silence.

Edson recognized the men. They'd been with Silvy Crawle the day he'd ridden into town, but Denver John wasn't there. Edson wasn't too surprised at that. Somehow he knew the gunman wasn't of bushwhack breed.

He looked around, stifled a smirk at the stamp of his would-be assailants. He wondered where Birdy and the other girls were. He guessed they were upstairs. Mainly because Midland would want few witnesses for his play.

'You ain't ever goin' to learn are you?' he challenged. 'You want to go on tuggin' my rope 'till I shoot the lot o' you?'

Midland moved forward away from the wall and Edson immediately slammed the shotgun across the counter top. The gambler jumped, held out his hands.

'You don't even breathe if you're goin' to wear a gun in front o' me,' Edson rasped at him. 'Get rid of your hardware now, or I'll bring the roof down on you.'

Midland's features were dark, twisted with helpless rage. 'Are you mad? You're never goin' to get out of Yellow Dog alive.'

Edson pushed the shotgun forward, hissed at the ominous click of the twin triggers. The men were up for a fight if a chance offered, but they read the look in Edson's eyes. They estimated they had little chance, put their guns onto nearby tables.

It was the shift in Midland's eyes that warned him. He'd forgotten Loomis. Too late, Edson saw the flash of movement as the barkeep flung a brass cuspidor along the back bar. It fell to the floor, bounced once and hit him in the side of his knee. White pain hit him and his leg buckled. He kneeled, cursing, and dropped the shotgun. He heard the yell of one of the gunmen and hurled the cuspidor back at Loomis, followed it up with a long desperate lunge. The barkeep twisted in a frantic effort to get away from behind the bar as Edson's hands found his throat. The marshal pounded Loomis's head against the damp floor until he felt the body crumple into oblivion. It was over in moments. He loosed his grip, tipped the foul contents of the cuspidor onto the unconscious barkeep.

He heard noise, knew the men were coming for him, probably from both ends of the bar. He lifted his Colt and fired at the brass lamp hanging from the ceiling above him. The bullet made a dull clang and immediately oil gouted in a thin stream. It fell to the counter, pooled and fell to Loomis's ashen face. As the light failed, another gun roared. Bottles and glasses, shelves and the mirror shattered above Edson.

He gritted his teeth against the pain in his leg, twisted and dived for the doorway through which he'd come. A bullet zipped past his head, splintered the doorjamb. Bending low he went through the doorway, stumbled and fell headlong into the darkness of Midland's room. Through the shouting in the saloon, he heard the gambler yell: 'Reckon you hit him, Po.'

Edson reached the open door at the rear of the building. Gasping at the searing pain in his leg, he stumbled into the night. But he was riding his luck. If they'd found the old shotgun had been loaded and in working order, he'd now be a crimson stain across the walls of Midland's room. He limped down the alley, back towards the main street. When he turned the corner to reach one of the saloon's dust-caked front windows he noticed the street was deserted. Even the coffin-maker and the pariah dogs knew well enough to stay away.

Through a chink in the shutters, in the deep gloom of the saloon, Edson saw the three gunmen watching Midland. He'd lit a bar lamp, was turning up the wick.

The first any of them knew of Edson's situation was when he fired from beneath the swing doors. The lamp on the bar was high and bright, silhouetting the men around it. They were all pointing guns wildly, as the one Midland had called Po collapsed like a punctured water bag. Edson's first and second bullets took him low in the belly. A second man was slammed back against the bar. He stared unsighted, fired into the wooden door slats above Edson's head. Then he took one step forward, fell onto a table with another .36 bullet deep in his chest.

Midland reached up and swept the

lamp off the counter, again plunged the saloon into blackness. Edson, crouched low, propelled himself headlong through the tables and chairs, broken glasses and spilled beer. He angled himself towards the far end of the bar where Loomis was still lying in a pool of spit and lamp-oil.

He fired again, in the direction of someone running. That wouldn't be Midland, he thought; must be the surviving Fat B gun. He pushed his Colt into his waistband, grabbed at the leg of a fallen chair. He arched his back, and with both hands heaved the chair across the room at the swing-doors. As it smashed into the woodwork, a sharp, bright flame blasted from close to where he guessed the remaining gunman to be. He pulled his Whitney, steadily fired his two remaining bullets. He heard the unmistakable muffled grunt, then the sigh of a stricken man. In the heavy silence that followed, he crawled forward. He touched the bar rail, and with his senses painful and sharp, he pulled himself to his feet.

To his right, the door to Midland's room slammed to. He pointed his gun with the spent chamber, as glasses crashed down from the bar top.

'Is that you, Loomis?' he rasped, ducking quickly.

'Don't shoot,' whined the barkeep. 'What the hell you done to me?'

'Light a lamp, or I'll come an' finish you off,' Edson snapped. Reloading, he backed off in the darkness, until his back was against a side wall. Then a match spluttered, and he saw Loomis's face. The man's hair was slicked to his wet skin, smeared across his glistening forehead. He grimaced, blinked against the hurt in his head and lit the lamp.

As the light grew, Edson looked around, covered the room with his gun. He swore violently at the mayhem. The man called Po was sitting on the floor, his back propped against the bar. His head rested on the front of his chest, his sightless eyes fixed on the dark jellied mess of his stomach. Near the centre of the room, another gunman lay prostrate across a flattened table. His face was twisted sideways, warped by an incredulous grin. The third gunman was staring at the darkened ceiling, the flat of one hand beating against the floor.

Edson limped forward.

'Go get the doc,' he told Loomis. Take your time. Get yourself cleaned up first.'

Edson picked up a table-lamp, watched Loomis sidle through the swing-doors. He pushed his way into Midland's room, knowing the gambler wouldn't be there. He wanted to drop the lamp, but thought of Birdy and the other girls in their rooms above. He turned down the light and moved back into the alleyway.

There were now a few inquisitive townsfolk gathered around and about the front of the saloon. Unrecognized, covered by the night, Edson limped off. He made his way across the street for Jasper's Hotel. His knee was a livid hurt and he felt a far-reaching tiredness.

Ten minutes later, with a soaked towel binding his swollen knee, he drifted into a fitful sleep. He heard loud noises from the street. Seemed to him, the whole town was milling beneath his open window.

It was long after sun-up when Edson rolled slowly, swung his legs over the edge of the bed. He swore, bent his knee and lumbered across the room to answer the door. Emmet Foyle stood on the narrow landing.

'There's a couple o' gentlemen. They're waitin' for you downstairs, Mr Ringer,' he said knowingly.

'What do *gentlemen* want with me'

The clerk coughed. 'Reckon it might have somethin' to do with a gunfight in the Broken Cage, last night. Mr Midland ain't too pleased.'

'He's lucky he's still alive,' Edson growled. 'Go tell 'em I'll be right down.'

Unhurried and careful Edson pulled on his boots. Then, carrying his gunbelt, he went down to the small lobby of the hotel. He saw Milo Treaves and Doc Pounce sitting either end of a crusty old sofa. Opposite them, Slick Midland sat in a slow-moving wooden rocker. In a corner of the lobby another man was sitting at a davenport. He appeared to be asleep, head down, on the desk top. His face was turned away, but there was something familiar about him.

With a slight limp, favouring one leg, Edson kept his eye on Midland as he crossed the lobby. He could see the gambler had a dark, swollen eye. It was set in a bluey puffed face above a fat upper lip.

He grunted recognition. 'Well, *gentlemen*, here I am' No one responded, so he turned to Midland. 'You look like you been bare-knucklin',' he commented.

'You made an almighty disturbance last night,' came back Treaves sharply. You shot three men . . . killed two of 'em'

'I'd o' made it four, if one of 'em hadn't lit out for the woods.' Edson glared at Midland.

'What'd I tell you?' Midland slurred. He turned to the doctor and Treaves. 'The man's a goddam killer. Where'd he come from, anyways?'

Pounce ignored him. 'Why don't you give us your version of what happened, Marshal?' he prompted.

Edson buckled on his gunbelt, told them how Loomis had called him over to the Broken Cage.

'Why'd you go through Slick's quarters, first?' the doc enquired.

'I was figurin' on comin' out again,' Edson explained briefly.

'I sent for the marshal. But he blew in like a norther . . . started shootin' the place up,' Midland blazed. 'Yeah, sure those Fat B men pulled their guns, but who'd blame 'em. It was self-defence.'

'I thought the law required guns to be checked,' Pounce said.

'They just rode in,' returned Midland.

Edson chuckled. 'You're so bent, you could spit fish-hooks,' he said.

Treaves huffed. He looked hard at Midland, then at Edson. 'I guess I'll he askin' you to turn in that star.'

'I already told you,' Edson said irately. 'You can have it when my month's up.'

'I don't see that Slick's explanation holds up any better than Edson's,' Pounce said. 'They were Jago Rizzle's gunmen in the bar, all right. But it seems to me there's a personal feud goin' on. Well I, for one, am stayin' clear.' With that, the doc nodded curtly at Edson and left the hotel.

'Don't forget a month's your limit, Marshal,' Treaves rumbled. He looked schemingly at Midland and the two men followed Pounce.

'Tut, tut, Marshal, you in trouble again?' The man who'd appeared to be taking a nap sat back and pushed his hat up. It was Parker Buck, 'You sure make more enemies than friends, friend. I hear there's odds of twenty to one against you making that pay-day.'

Edson looked curiously at Buck, who started to rub the knuckles of his right hand.

'Didn't know you were back. You get to hear what happened to Midland's face?'

Buck grinned roguishly. 'Let's just say, I caught him doin' something I didn't like . . . somethin' he won't be too quick to shout about,' he said.

10

Run From Yellow Dog

As was required of the marshal, Edson made the rounds of Yellow Dog at sundown. He was going it alone now, now that Treaves had shown his true hand. Edson knew the man's businesses would suffer if Jago Rizzle's gunhands ran wild through the town. But if it was a choice between law and order and money?

Edson though was more worried about Birdy; had been since he'd gone back to the Broken Cage. Uneasy and concerned, his pace quickened. He cursed himself for not checking on her welfare, woke in a sweat during the early hours thinking about it.

Nothing seemed wrong or out of order when he stepped between the saloon's brea flares. The piano was banging out a popular folk tune. Two cowboys were swinging their girls and two others were laughing, stomping together. Loomis, his neck bruised from Edson's grip, was pouring beer for a few drinkers at the bar. From around the card-table, Slick Midland looked up. On seeing Edson, he blinked, turned back to his cards. But his jaw twitched. Suddenly his mind wasn't on the dealt hands any more.

Edson went straight to the bar.

'Is Dove around?' he asked Loomis.

'Who's askin' . . . the marshal or Mr Ringer?' Without waiting for a response, Loomis continued: 'She's sick.' The way Edson was looking at him, he faltered: 'Been in her bed.'

Edson knew he'd lied, was already making for the stairs.

'Hey, you can't go up there, it's the private — '

'Come and stop me,' Edson flung back.

At the top of the stairway the landing was lit by four bracketed wall lamps.

Edson swore at the heady cloy of cheap perfume and beer. He heard a woman's voice and then a man's from one of the rooms. He moved to the left, started when a door opened and a girl poked her head out.

'Where's Dove's room?' he asked her.

'At the end.'

Edson found the door, tried the door-handle tentatively, but it was locked. He knocked and waited, knocked again. Nothing. With his usual vigour he took one step back and kicked the door open. The door splintered, crashed in, and in the blackness of the room he called Birdy's name.

'You here, Birdy. It's me. Eddie.'

Wary of a trap, Edson turned, lifted one of the landing lamps off its bracket. Holding it high and out front, he peered back into the room. He saw Birdy lying on a narrow cot, her face blotchy, puffed from an obvious beating. But her eyes bulged bright and wet when they met his. She had a coverlet drawn across her and for a moment didn't, couldn't move. Edson pounded with anger. Then, with a bitter curse, he stepped forward. He rested the lamp on the floor and attempted to raise her shoulders. With a sharp intake of breath, Birdy flinched.

'He beat me up good, Eddie.'

'Midland?' he asked, knowing the answer, knowing the man was playing poker below.

'Yeah. Seems like you made him mad . . . real mad.' Birdy mouthed the words, her swollen lips moving painfully.

'Me? What does he know about me . . . you an' me?'

'Someone saw us . . . that night you . . . he reckons we know each other, talkin' intimate like. He wanted to know what . . . what I know about you.' Birdy smiled weakly. 'I never told him, Eddie.'

'No. The Birdy I know, wouldn't. I'm sorry for that Birdy . . . what I done. I'll get Doc Pounce over here, straight away. You'll be all right.'

Edson saw doors quickly close as he made it to the stairs, down the steps two, three at a time. He glared around him.

'You know who I want. Where is he?'

'He's gone,' one of the card-players said. With a nod, the man indicated the door to Midland's room. 'He got flustered when you started kicking the place apart.'

Edson turned back to Loomis. 'Go get the doc. Tell him Birdy . . . Dove's hurt bad. It ain't a request.'

Edson stood outside the door to Midland's room and shook his head, knew he was about two or three minutes too late. He twisted the door-handle and slowly drew the door open. As he thought: light falling from the saloon showed the room to be empty. Midland hadn't wasted any time. He'd probably guessed what was coming, had made arrangements.

Edson went through the room into the alley, round and out onto the plankwalk at the front of the building. He stood and listened, heard the creak and groan, the snap of traces. It was the ill-famed River Line mail coach, leaving on its overnight stage to Grey Dog, Glenn's Ferry and eventually, Boise. Slick Midland would be on board. He had either gambler's luck or timing.

Edson ran to the south end of town. It took him thirty seconds to make the yellow-and-black-painted stage depot. The agent seemed to be waiting, was standing in the doorway.

'Slick Midland haul out?' he yelled.

'Yep, Marshal. Said he'd mail back the fare. You'd o' thought his life depended on it.'

'It did. It did.' Edson spat into the ground, turned back to the Broken Cage.

Birdy was propped up. Doc Pounce had soothed the abrasions, given her a sedative. He turned as Edson came into the room, held up his hand. 'You know it's *after* the danger that everyone's wise,' he commented.

'Yeah, I know. It won't happen again,' Edson said sincerely.

'Did you get him?' Birdy asked, her voice a little stronger.

'Nope. With a good mount, maybe I could o' got to him somewhere before Snake Pass. But he can wait. I wanted to see you, Birdy.'

'Do you know where he's goin', Eddie?'

'Nope. Payette maybe. Somewhere where there's a real deep hole in the border trash. Is she all right, Doc? Nothin' too long lastin'?'

Pounce was clearly surprised at the association of Marshal Ringer and Dove. 'No. She'll mend. She needs a rest from her work downstairs though.'

'She'll get it,' Edson told the doctor, who believed him and smiled cautiously.

Edson had to get Birdy out of the Broken Cage. But where could she go? Where could he take her? He knew that the best doors would remain closed to any saloon girl. Except

121

Jasper's Hotel, maybe?

Within minutes, the marshal's sharp rap on the desk brought Emmet Foyle to his senses.

'I want a room. A room for a woman,' Edson said.

Foyle mouthed the word, 'woman'.

'Sorry . . . lady. It's Miss Dove from the Broken Cage.'

'Yeah, I know her, but we ain't got no rooms available.'

'The place's half empty, Foyle, you know it.'

'I'm sorry, Marshal,' Foyle stuttered. 'It's just that management policy states — '

'Management policy,' Edson echoed aloud. 'I thought that's what *you* were. Who owns this place?'

'Mr Treaves.'

'Yeah, I should o' guessed. I'll give you my month's pay for a room, you miserable son-of-a-bitch.'

Foyle shook his head sadly. 'I'm sorry. I need my job here, Marshal. Mr Treaves would see me on the street for lettin' her . . . Miss Dove in.'

Edson knew that Foyle wasn't a bad man. But if he told him about Birdy, the whole town would hear before midnight that he was Eddie Riner, Bur Blacksmith's killer come back.

Edson's eyes drilled coldly into Foyle while he considered the situation. There was another option. He could ask Estrella Mace. She might be priggish, pious maybe, but he could take advantage of that. She'd want to be seen doing the proper thing; taking in the 'soiled sister'.

So he went to the western outskirts where, among other things, Milo Treaves told him she had a house among the willows, bankside to a branch of Goose Creek.

'Why, Marshal Ringer!' she exclaimed. 'What can I do for you at this hour?'

Edson pulled off his hat, stood awkwardly. 'I came to thank you for offerin' to help with the papers . . . the office records, ma'am.'

'No you didn't, Marshal. What is it

you really want?'

Edson puffed his cheeks, blew air through his lips. 'It's Miss Dove, ma'am . . . from the er . . . Broken Cage. Do you know her?'

'I don't *know* her. Know *of* her . . . yes. Why?'

'She needs a room.'

'A room! What has that got to do with *me*, Marshal?'

Edson gritted his teeth in a thin smile, cursed quietly without moving his lips. 'I thought maybe you could put her up. Find room for a few days?'

Estrella Mace appeared to be horrified. 'You want me to — '

'I got to get her out of the saloon, ma'am,' Edson interrupted. 'She's been beaten bad. Nowhere else will take her in. I thought, maybe you could.'

'Then thinking along those lines is not your strong point,' Estrella Mace told him. She shook her head violently, anger almost stifling her words. 'No, she can't come here,' she said and shut the door.

11

Moving Along

From behind the door, Estrella Mace
fought ineffectively to walk away. She
closed her eyes, and bit her lip. Then
she opened the door again. The marshal
was standing by a fence-post, looking
back at her.

'It's a fine night,' he said.

Estrella Mace smiled compliantly.
'Go and get her,' she said. 'I have a
spare room.'

'Thank you, but maybe I shouldn't
have asked. It won't do your reputation
any good, will it?'

'Good teachers should be good
learners, Marshal. Furthermore, I
wouldn't be living or working in this
godforsaken part of the world unless I
had the courage to do what *I* thought
was right.'

'You ain't worried about losing that work, ma'am?'

'If the bigots of Yellow Dog want themselves a new schoolteacher, they can go and get one. Now, why don't you go and get Miss Dove. I'll make a room over.' With that, Estrella Mace turned back into her house.

At Stryder's Livery, Edson requisitioned a buckboard, drove it to the Broken Cage. A hasty silence imbued the saloon when he entered and he went straight for the stairs. One of the other girls who was sitting beside Birdy got up, left the room with an understanding, considerate smile.

'How you doin', kid?' he asked.

'How'd you feel if some lunkhead had beat you like a floor-rug?'

'Hmm. Well, I'm movin' you out of this joint,' Edson said.

'Yeah. I'd rather bed down with Stryder's horses than stay here another minute.'

'No, Birdy. You'll be with Miss Mace . . . the school-ma'am.'

126

'You joshin' me, Eddie? Why, she wouldn't touch the likes o' me with a pig-sticker.'

'No? Well she's fixin' you a room right now; makin' it real pretty.'

'You got a wanted dodger out on her, Eddie?'

'No, Birdy. She's just a very fine lady. She's got a kind face too, if you look beyond the cover-up.' Edson laughed, was helping Birdy up from her cot when Parker Buck shadowed the doorway.

'You movin' out? he asked of the marshal.

'Hey, Buck!' Edson welcomed. 'If you're stayin' around long enough, make yourself useful. Roll all Birdy's war paint into a sheet, an' them dresses. Bring it all over to the schoolma'am's house, will you?'

'Yessir, Marshal. The town's goin' to love this. Keep their tongues a waggin'.'

Again the saloon was smothered by unease and discomfiture. The patrons watched Edson slowly descend the stairs with Birdy, cross the saloon floor. At the swing-doors, Birdy couldn't resist a final gesture. Her bruised features twisted into the semblance of a smile.

'Goodbye, boys. Don't forget me,' she slurred through stinging lips.

'Where you goin', Sweet Dove?' a gruff voice enquired.

'To get me some learnin'.'

'That can't be much . . . wouldn't amount to more'n lark-spit,' was the response, and immediately a few men started in on their own brand of feral humour. It took a menacing glare from Edson to crush the ensuing guffaws.

Twenty minutes after Edson and Birdy left the saloon, Jago Rizzle arrived. It was a tentative arrival, although he rode in with his habitual escort of gunmen. He wanted to mix it at the bar, wanted to know how his reputation fared, how he stood after having two of his gunmen shot dead by the marshal. Like most of the towns-folk, he was more than surprised to find out that the Broken Cage's Sweet Dove was recuperating under the wing of the town's schoolteacher.

★ ★ ★

That same schoolteacher was sitting in a rocker, watching and listening to the tick of her mantel clock. It was way beyond her usual turning-in time, but she was too agitated for sleep. In just a few hours, the train of another dull and dreary evening had been completely derailed.

Then she heard the sound of a footfall on the stoop, flinched at the tap on the door that followed. She rubbed her tired eyes, wondered about answering the door at 2.15 in the morning, even to the marshal. Oh, what the hell, she thought daringly and got up to brighten the lamp.

But it wasn't Edson Ringer.

Jago Rizzle removed his Stetson, nodded courteously when the door opened.

'Miss Mace?' he enquired of her. 'My name's Rizzle . . . Jago Rizzle. He smiled. 'You won't know me. I guess our trails don't meet,' He almost winked, smiled again.

'What can I do for you, Mr Rizzle? You know we're actually two or three hours away from daybreak?'

'Yes, ma'am, I'm sorry. But I understand a very good friend of mine . . . Miss Dove, is stayin' with you.'

'Indeed she is, yes.'

'I didn't know you two knew each other?'

'I don't. I agreed that she's staying with me. It was a request from Marshal Ringer.'

Rizzle nodded. 'I see,' he said. 'So the marshal knows her then, does he?'

Estrella already knew the answer to that. 'I guess he does', she affirmed. 'You'd best ask him. But what do you want?'

'Well, I'd like to see her . . . Dove. As I said, I'm a close friend.'

'Where's your sense Mr Rizzle? You

certainly can't see her until tomorrow. If then.'

Rizzle took a small step back. 'I see. Yes, of course. Please tell her that I called. And if there's anything . . . please let me know.'

'I will. Thank you, and goodnight, Mr Rizzle.'

More disturbed, Estrella Mace stood in the doorway, watched Rizzle lead off his blood bay. She *had* heard of Jago Rizzle, owner of the combined Fat B and Rolling Post ranches.

A couple of hours earlier, Edson had explained how he knew Birdy, about Ma Gracey and the loggers' cabin. He told her of Bur Blackrule, the shooting, his years away. The schoolteacher was glad. She also hoped that any speculation on Rizzle's part would be compromised by his relationship with Birdy, and that he'd probably keep quiet.

Jago Rizzle walked his horse back to the Broken Cage. His mind was racing with his new-found suspicion.

'I got it. I know'd I'd seen him somewhere before,' he rasped into the night. 'Our newly appointed town marshal's a grown up Eddie Riner. Methinks I'll get a note off to the county sheriff before I put my own butt in danger again. Let Cole Morelock do it. Goddammit, Riner's still carryin' the same primitive cannon.' Rizzle was so vehement, his horse nickered, crowhopped anxiously.

12

Night Mail

After an early plate of Johan Gries's fried pork and warm biscuits, Edson sat at his office desk. He sipped coffee, stared thoughtfully out of the fly-specked window. Late last night he'd seen Parker Buck and Jago Rizzle in the gloom of the alley alongside the Broken Cage.

There was nothing wrong with Buck's talking with Rizzle, but it didn't shape up with the marshal. Why would a 'saddlebum' be meeting secretly with the biggest cowman along Snake River? Edson chewed it over for a while, before his thoughts drifted to Estrella Mace.

As if on cue, the schoolma'am appeared shortly after.

'Good morning, Marshal,' she said formally. 'I've brought a message from

Dove. She says it's most important that she sees you. Please hurry.' Then she was gone.

Ten minutes later, Edson let himself in to Estrella Mace's house. Birdy was waiting, standing outside the room she'd been using.

'What's wrong?' he said. 'You got trouble?'

'No, you have. Rizzle's goin' to figure out who you are.'

'How'd you make that out, kid?'

'From what Estrella told me. He called here early this morning . . . wanted to see me. Estrella thinks he guessed it right off'

'Why would Rizzle come here?'

'Why'd you think, Eddie? You've been around some.'

Edson's jaw dropped. 'He's married, Birdy . . . to Katey Cate. You must know that?'

'You ought to ride swing on the moral stuff, Eddie . . . just get out o' town.'

Slow and uncertain, Edson shook his

head. 'I don't think so, Birdy. Rizzle ain't goin' to get much done. County sheriff can't get here before sundown. That gives me nearly twelve hours. How much did you tell Miss Mace, or should I say, Estrella?'

'Nothin'. She don't know any more'n you told her, Eddie.'

Edson looked nonplussed. 'You'll leave here . . . go back to the Broken Cage?'

'Me goin' back *there*'s no worse than you ever comin' back *here*. I'm sorry, Eddie, but you've caused enough trouble. Now please just go. Leave town.'

★ ★ ★

Edson went straight to the coach station and questioned the agent.

'Jago Rizzle been here? Or anyone else who sent messages up to Boise?'

'No, Marshal. An' no one's mailed anythin' west o' Glenn's Ferry,' the man lied.

135

But the news took the edge off Edson's concern; made him think he'd have another full day before he'd have to ride out of Yellow Dog.

The agent's hands were sweating. He knew full well that word had been sent to Sheriff Cole Morelock. He'd seen Rizzle write the note; remembered vividly how it had told of Marshal Edson Ringer being Eddie Riner. The killer of Bur Blackrule had returned to the scene of his crime. The agent was worried, knew what would happen if the marshal found out he knew of the communication. Still, it was exciting. Maybe Ringer would hole up for a shoot-out in Jasper's Hotel. Oh yes. Milo Treaves sure cracked a bone when he handed out the lawman's badge.

Edson got the grey mare back from Stryder's Livery. He rode slowly down the main street, saw Parker Buck slouched outside Diggers' Moon.

'Hey, Edson, you thought any more about turnin' in that badge?' Buck asked enigmatically.

Edson was surprised. If Buck was in cahoots with Rizzle, he'd be playing to keep him in town until Rizzle returned with the sheriff. This was a good chance to call his hand.

'Funny . . . it's what I'm thinkin' right now,' he drawled. 'Could be I'll mosey along with you, Parker. Do some trail findin'. I heard they want to cut the north run from Brigham City.'

Parker Buck ran a calculating eye over him. 'Short month eh?' he said sarcastically.

'It keeps the enemy guessin' an' I always was an unpredictable son-of-a-gun,' he returned with an edge.

Buck stretched. 'Yeah, you an' me both. How soon can you leave?'

* * *

The sun was approaching its zenith. It burned the plain with a vengeance when the two men drummed across one of two wooden bridges that spanned Goose Creek. They were

137

headed west for Glenn's Ferry and beyond.

Edson squirmed under the heat, tried to ease his sweaty shirt from his back.

'We should've pulled out at sun-up,' he said.

Parker grunted. 'At sun-up tomorrow mornin', you'd have been in the hoosegow, probably wearin' leg-irons.'

'Hoosegow . . . leg-irons! What the hell you talkin' about?'

'Jago Rizzle sent word to the county sheriff last night.'

Edson blanched. 'What's that got to do with me?' he asked unconvincingly.

'Word says you're that Eddie Riner they been lookin' for, for five years.'

'Six!' Edson corrected, and made a move for his Colt.

'Hold up,' Parker said, startled. 'Jeez, I ain't goin' to hold a killin' against you. You couldn't o' been much more'n a weaner.'

Edson thought fast. If the roving trail finder hadn't suggested they ride out of town immediately, the sheriff would

138

have had him dead in the water. But Parker had known of Rizzle's scheme. That was surely proof enough they were working together.

'What kind of a hand you playing, Parker?' he lead with.

Parker shrugged. 'Not sure. Could be that in Snake River territory you ain't such a bad companion; as long as you're packin' that old Colt.'

Edson heeled his mare and they cantered west. 'I never beefed Bur Blackrule,' he said after a while. Then he told of his encounter with Jimson Bench in Grey Dog and his talk with Trimmer Fogg, the intrigue of the .36 and .45-calibre slugs.

'You say this Bur Blackrule was standin' up on steps of his house? You aimed at his feet?' queried Parker.

'*Between* his feet. I couldn't . . . didn't miss.'

Parker thought for a moment. I'm ridin' to the Fat B,' he said. 'If you want to stay clear o' Morelock, ride to that pass you been tellin' me about.

We'll meet up there.'

'What do you want out at the Fat B?'

'To see if they object to trail drives crossin' their range, o' course. That's what I get paid for. When they say no, I'll start diggin' around for somethin' else.' Parker tapped the side of his nose, laughed mysteriously.

Uneasily, Edson watched horse and rider until they were no more than tiny, shimmering spectres on the horizon. Was Parker Buck dealing from the bottom, he wondered. Was it the man's intention to deliver him up to Rizzle? Maybe Parker figured on cutting into the blood money that was even now available. Hell, he thought. Six years later and he was still running.

Head down, his horse plugged on towards Squirrel Gap.

13

Checking Out

When Parker Buck rode into the Fat B yard it was mid-afternoon and the ranch appeared to be deserted. He dismounted at the trough, watered his horse and eyed the quiet spread. A tendril of smoke drifted from the chimney of the cooking-shack. He walked over and pushed the door open. A man was sitting on an upturned flour barrel, shucking corn.

'Jago around? Parker inquired.

'Who's askin'?'

'Parker Buck. Land agent.' Parker stretched the truth.

'Oh. Well, he's gone to Yellow Dog. Gone with a few of his gunnies.' With distaste, the cooker-man pitched more corn into a water pail. 'Must be somethin' goin' on.' He nodded at the coffee-pot on the stove. 'Stay awhile. Pour yourself a mug.'

When he'd finished his coffee, Parker said thanks and wandered outside. Unhurried, he looked over the bunk-house, ranch buildings and the main house. He saw the wide porch that spanned its front, the six wooden steps that led up to the veranda. It was where Bur Blackrule had stood six years before. Parker missed nothing, not even the snubbed barrel of a wood rifle that nosed around the angle of the house.

'Grab some sky, mister.' A small, well-dusted boy crawled into view. He was squinting, screwing up his nose as he raised the gun.

Parker flung up his arms. 'You got the drop on me. Don't shoot,' he drawled.

The kid scrambled to his feet He was about four, was clad in bib overalls. 'You'm a ring-toter.' His eyes were bright and excited.

'Nope. Never took a steer in my life, pard. I come here peaceful,' Parker assured him. 'Can I drop my hands?'

'Yep. But stay clear o' your gun. I'm guardin' the Fat B.'

Parker waved the kid away. 'Your pa needs to get you to bed earlier,' he said quietly. He moved to the house, had a thorough look at the front of the steps and the risers. He pulled out a clasp knife and began to jab at the wood. He was prising out a shapeless lump of lead from near the top when a startled shout stopped him.

'What're you doing. Who are you?' a young woman demanded, naturally annoyed.

Parker smiled his best smile. 'Tryin' to stop an innocent man from hanging', ma'am.'

'What are you talking about? This is my ranch.'

Parker dropped the old bullet into his shirt pocket. 'I know that, ma'am. It's a long story, but it's real enough, an' right here's where it started.'

Intrigued, her manner questioning, she leaned against the porch rail. 'Make the story a short one before I call for help.'

Parker moved down a step, in a few words related the story.

'I met a feller . . . name of Edson Ringer. Told me how he wanted to shoot up the boots of Bur Blackrule. But seems like he missed . . . by a good yard. Ended up on the run for six years.'

The lady started to shake her head slowly. 'I . . . I'm sorry, I don't . . . I mean, I do but . . . '

'Yeah, it's hard to figure, ma'am, unless you happen to know that when they dug the slug out of Blackrule, it was found to be a .45. Edson Ringer packed a .36. I got his bullet with me. Seems like he didn't miss after all.'

The girl was in control, but slightly shocked. You're talking about Eddie, aren't you? Eddie Riner?'

'Yes, ma'am. He calls himself Edson Ringer now.'

'I was here . . . standing . . . I saw him shoot. There was only the one shot

. . . I remember. I'll never forget. Eddie knew he'd killed Bur. That's why he ran. Are you saying . . . '

'I'm sayin' he made the same mistake you did,' Parker said. 'Eddie Riner, as he was then, didn't hear any second shot either. He figured his gun threw high. For six years he's been thinkin' on that . . . dodgin' a murder warrant for someone else's killin'.'

There was awakened interest in the girl's eyes, but her voice was doubtful.

'Are you sure . . . about Eddie carrying a .36?'

'Yes, ma'am. No reason to doubt him. Not after diggin' the slug out from where I just did.'

'I often wondered . . . ' she started to say, the words drifting off.

'It could have been a rifle . . . a Winchester,' Parker murmured. 'The bullet that did for Blackrule.' He turned, eyed the land beyond the yard and home pasture.

'A Winchester you say? Just a moment.' The lady came down the steps towards him, pulled open the door to the storm cellar. Parker looked around for the kid, waited until she reappeared with a tarnished and neglected Winchester.

'I picked this out of the creek after Bur was killed . . . about a month after. I thought it was Eddie's . . . that he'd brought it with him. It's been in the cellar all this time. I don't think anyone else knew about it.'

Parker took the gun. The action grated, but a spent case fell to the ground. 'Yeah, that's a .45,' he said, stooping to pick it up. 'You've taken good care o' the evidence, ma'am. Reckon this exhibit's what killed Bur Blackrule.'

'If it wasn't Eddie's, whose could it be?'

Understandingly, Parker shrugged. 'At this moment, that's anybody's guess, ma'am. Reckon I'll be takin' it along though.'

The lady nodded her assent, started considering the circumstances. 'Who are you?' she asked. 'Are you a friend of Eddie's?'

'The answer to that, ma'am, is, I could well be, an' Parker Buck's the name.' Parker touched his hat as lie bade farewell, smiled politely. 'Good day, ma'am. Be sure to tell your husband that I passed this way.'

★   ★   ★

Its head dipping, the grey mare laboured along the covert trail that slanted up to the cleft in the timberline that was Squirrel Gap. Hidden among the stands of pine, Edson drew rein beside a small, dark pool. Behind it rose a sheer wall of rock at the footings of the Raft River mountains; thick vegetation rimmed the bank where Edson dismounted. He'd given precise details on the location, so hours later he didn't do more than draw back the hammer of the Whitney at the sound of the rider approaching. With his other hand he casually reached for the coffee-can, as

147

Parker Buck rode in.

Parker looked around him, blew an appreciative whistle.

'I'd say you're in the clear for Blackrule's killin',' he said straight off, climbing wearily from his saddle.

Edson swirled the hot, stewed coffee.

'Well that's good news after six years. How'd you know it?'

'I dug out your .36 slug. It was right where it would o' been if you'd told me the truth of it . . . and you did.'

Edson handed over his coffee. 'How can you prove that piece o' lead's mine?'

'I can't.'

'Well ain't that just dandy. A find that's about as much use as wet wood. What did Rizzle have to say? You must've seen him?

'No, he was in town, an' you can guess why? Met his wife though, an' his kid. Nice folk.' Parker looked around him. This is a real fresh spot, Edson.'

'Yeah. I've know'd it for years. There's not many others do though.'

His head against a grassy tuft, Parker stretched out, contemplated the coffee. 'I met a cowpoke somewhere down near the creek,' he said after a few moments. 'He was tellin' me one o' the ranches lost a hundred head last night. Small spread . . . means a lot to 'em.' The trail finder looked over at Edson. 'I reckon they're hidden in this neck o' the woods if they're to be driven north. What do you say?'

'Yeah, an' there's only one place I know of. It's just east o' here . . . back below the timberline.'

'I'd like to take a look. Sun-up tomorrow,' Parker suggested.

Edson had been meaning to ask his companion something since they'd cut from Yellow Dog. He thought now was the time.

'Say Parker,' he said, 'What *is* it, you an' Jago Rizzle been hatchin' up? I seen the two o' you together, an' I got the strange feelin' it should concern me?' he calmly insinuated.

Slowly, Parker rolled onto his side,

set his coffee down.

'What reason you got to think that, Edson?' he enquired with a lean smile.

'Five hundred dollars' bounty, that's what.'

'Hah. If I'd wanted five hundred that bad, I'd o' taken it in town. Not run the risk o' losin' you out here, you dumb cluck.'

'What you cosyin' up to Rizzle for? I saw you, last night?' Edson snapped back.

Understanding dawned in Parker's eyes. 'I'm trail findin'. I really was goin' to ask about crossin' his land. I figured maybe he'd agree, seein' as how he's a member of the Snake River Cattlemen's Protective.'

'What's so secretive about that?'

Parker sniggered. 'He needs talkin' round. The ring-toters been givin' him trouble too. I'm concerned about that, but I don't want anyone thinkin' him an' me are buddies.'

'Yeah, well that's as maybe,' Edson said, unconvinced. He yawned. 'Maybe it'll sound better in the mornin'.'

An hour later, as the moon silvered the rim of the Rafters, a lone timber wolf sloped up to the edge of the pool. It took a bellyful of water, stared defiantly at the men before fading back into the darkness of the pines. Edson couldn't sleep. He lay staring up at the stars, tried to figure out Parker Buck.

14

In Hiding

In the chill of dawn the two men saddled up and rode east. As the sky lightened, they stayed mostly hidden along the timberline, away from inquisitive eyes, the rising fire of the sun.

Every hour the riders dismounted, spilled water from their canteens into their hats to give their horses a brief drink. But long before noon, the horses were dehydrated, their coats glistening with sweat

'I'd say it ain't rained here since they floated the Ark,' Parker suggested, peering across the shimmering heat haze.

'I'd say it's savin' itself,' came back Edson. He thought back to the storm of six years ago, when he stood in Bur Blackrule's yard. He climbed into the saddle, led off west again. After an hour they dropped from the timberline, moved slightly north. The heat intensified, burned off gully walls as they headed into the western stretch of Snake Plain. Sweat soaked their clothing, stung their eyes.

Eventually, beneath the overhang of a piny ridge, Edson checked his mount and stepped down. 'You carryin' a spyglass?' he asked Parker.

Parker nodded, dismounted and pulled at the straps of a saddlebag. Together they clambered up the steep, rocky escarpment. When they reached the crest, they bellied down, crawled through the skimpy line of trees.

Below them a narrow gulch stretched ahead. Its poor soil was near barren, pitted only with creosote and scrub pine. But near the far end, cheat grass added a touch of life. Criss-crossing the gulch, and shadowed dark against the arid soil, a small herd grazed, and a lone rider circled it.

'Jeez!' Parker uttered. 'You certainly

know where the action is in this territory, Edson.' He brought up his 'scope, adjusted the focus. 'There's a corral . . . a brandin' chute on the far side,' he said.

'That'd be the cattle taken from the Goose Creek ranchers. I'd say more'n a hundred head,' Edson confirmed.

Parker continued to study the rustlers' camp for a moment, then he glanced sideways at Edson as he spoke. 'I sure ain't goin' to split my skin ridin' back to Yellow Dog. We'll rush 'em after sundown. In the dark, two against five's a piece o' piss, Edson.'

'Yeah, I guess it is,' Edson affirmed uncertainly. 'But I don't understand why we're gettin' involved.'

Parker closed his telescope and they wormed their way back from the ridge. 'I work for the Cattlemen's Protective,' he answered breathlessly. 'This'll do me some good. Maybe even get me a reward from those that're losin' beeves.'

★ ★ ★

Through the dense creosote, Edson watched four men as they hunkered around their camp fire. Yellow and orange flame licked into the night, shone upon strained faces, wary eyes. Some way behind Edson, the night guard lay gagged and trussed across a scrub pine.

Slowly, Edson crawled closer, then waited for Parker's show from the other side of the camp. It came after another long five minutes.

'Raise your hands boys. Do it real slow.'

The rustlers' murmured talk choked off. Only the eyes of the small group of men moved, searching the darkness. From outside the circle of firelight, Edson moved forward, cracked through a thin carpet of burned up desert weed.

'You heard the man,' he barked. 'Stretch 'em upwards.'

But the rustlers chose another way. They threw themselves into reckless, guilt-ridden action by going for their guns. Lead whined and whistled as they triggered at shadowy forms. Edson's Colt was bucking, spouting fire as Parker went into action from the brush beyond.

Outlined by their own camp-fire, the rustlers were clear targets while Edson and Parker were cloaked by the night. Lead smashed into one man and embers sparked and showered as he crashed across the burning brushwood. Another managed to get to his feet before Parker's bullet sent him staggering sideways, dead before he went down again. The two others yelled as they dropped their guns, raised their arms high.

Parker walked into the firelight, smoking gun levelled menacingly. 'Get their guns,' he shouted.

Edson picked up the rustlers' guns, noticed they were the usual cowmen's cheap imitations. Then he dragged the dead man from the fire, swore with disgust at the smouldering body. While Parker covered the other two men, he kicked the remaining ash into a pile, tossed on some trampled brush. Flame spouted again, and in its light Edson noted with some surprise that one of the two men was wounded. He was an older man, certainly old enough to be the father of any of them.

He stood watching, gave the hatless, grey-haired rustler time to wrap a dirty neckerchief around his bloody forearm. Then he helped Parker rope them both to an upright of the makeshift corral.

'I'll go get the one you took care of.' Parker offered.

Edson stepped close to the wounded rustler. 'What's your name, feller?' he demanded.

'What's it matter?'

'There's a few ranchers'll want to know. You want a bullet in the other arm?' Edson warned.

'Bramwell Mace,' the man said, sullenly.

'Mace?' Edson repeated. 'You related to the schoolma'am in Yellow Dog?'

The man said nothing, but Edson

could see the answer written large across his face, as well as in his grey eyes. Edson swore with incredulity, immediately considered the standing of Estrella. He shook his head, swore again. Along with Doctor Pounce, Estrella Mace was just about the only other person in town with both professional and social status. What a day of cheerless mockery they'd have when her father was brought in to face a charge of cattle-rustling.

Edson backed off. His mind was still racing when Parker returned with the rustler who'd been the night guard. His arms were folded around a creosote stick and tied securely behind his back.

'Get down,' Parker snarled, pushing the man towards his two colleagues.

After dragging the bodies of the two dead men out into the brush, Edson and Parker kneeled beside the fire. Parker was settling from the gunfight, his spirits improving.

'Never figured on a break like this,' said Parker. 'We got all of 'em I reckon

. . . well nearly. And then there's the stock to return. It makes a change from beatin' a trail north in the name o' herd owners. These gents'll be sweatin' it out so long in Yuma, they'll be playin' cradle with their whiskers.'

'What do you mean . . . 'nearly'? Edson asked thoughtfully. 'You know of someone else?'

'There's always someone else, Edson. These birds take orders . . . they don't give 'em.' Parker raised his voice for the benefit of the miserable rustlers. 'Yuma ain't no plush Eastern hotel. I'd sure sing a sweet song to keep out o' that joint.'

Edson said nothing about Parker's hinting. He was thinking of Estrella Mace. She was risking her livelihood, her good name, to help him keep Birdy from the Broken Cage saloon. Nevertheless, soon after they hit town, Yellow Dog would be sending to Denver for a new schoolteacher. Edson spat into the fire. Hell, he thought. What a way to say thank you; putting her pa behind bars.

Parker broke into his silent concern. 'Toss you for first sleep,' he said, pulling a coin, spinning it high. 'You lose,' he decided. He moved into the darkness, returned a few minutes later with their traps and bedrolls. Edson was still staring into the fire when Parker slid beneath his slicker.

Five minutes later the troubled Edson got up and walked over to the captives. He made out their dark forms, the whites of their eyes. Two of them sagged back against their secure tying. Mace continued to stare at Edson, his face haggard, ghostly pale.

Edson stepped in close, leaned to make pretence of inspecting the rope that tied the man's wrists. With a quick glance in Parker's direction, he hissed out his instructions. 'I'm goin' to cut the rope, not your neck . . . so keep quiet.'

The old rustler thought for a moment, then made a guttural laughing sound. 'Yeah, the trigger itch, Marshal. No thanks, Ringer, we all heard o' you.'

Edson smiled bleakly. 'I wouldn't waste a bullet on an old rooster like you. I'd just wring it's neck. I'm doin' this to get me some favour with your — ' Edson thought better of what he was going to say. 'Don't stop 'til you get to Oregon,' he said instead.

He severed the ropes, and Mace climbed unsteadily to his feet. The man looked hard at Edson. 'I know you from somewhere kid,' he said, uncertainly and slowly. Then he rubbed his wrists, nodded briefly and was gone towards his horse and the north end of the near-barren gulch.

Almost immediately, Parker was shouting. Edson was thrown against the corral post as, gun in hand, the trail finder charged past him into the night. Edson knew then the wise thing to do would be to go after Mace. Parker couldn't follow, not with a brace of trussed rustlers. Then his dilemma was settled; Parker had outsmarted him. The man had fired off a couple of shots into the night while running in a tight circle. Edson felt the gun muzzle nudging into the small of his back.

'You'd never've made it as a lawman,' Parker snorted. 'That ol' critter's made it away with his own horse an' rifle.'

Edson stood still, felt his Colt being lifted from his holster.

'At least you ain't causin' me any more trouble,' Parker advised him.

*　*　*

A miserable party wound its way back to the timberline of the Rafters and Squirrel Gap. Under the blue cloudless sky, Parker took the lead, his slicker-roll stuffed with rifles, his saddle horn looped with gunbelts. Behind him trailed three horses, each with a bound prisoner in the saddle. In the rear trudged the rustled steers. He knew they'd follow the horses.

Edson hung his head in the oppressive, unrelenting heat. For him, it seemed like the end. At Yellow Dog, Cole Morelock's posse probably awaited him. With the charge of murder tagged on to his part in working Mace's escape, it would mean the rope. At best, a life's term in Yuma. The notoriety though would at least secure him a banner headline, column inches in the Snake River Gazette. He remembered telling Ma Gracey that he'd be back one day: now he laughed bleakly at the quirk of fate.

He blinked hard, squeezed his eyes shut against the overhead sun and the run of sweat. Then he flinched at the sound of a rifleshot that split the searing air.

15

Cut Loose

Ahead of Edson, Parker Buck's horse snorted once, then collapsed in a dreadful flurry of stones and dust.

The horses with roped men in the saddles bunched in confusion around the stricken animal. Parker was desperately wrenching his left leg from under the horse's flank. He got free, stumbled to his feet. Then again the hidden gun threw lead. Parker was pulling a rifle from his slicker-roll, when he was hit. He staggered, looked around him, astonished, with blood trickling down the side of his forehead. Then he groaned, dropped and lay prone beside his mount.

Edson gulped, his breathing suddenly uncontrollable and heavy. He shook his head and cursed as realization took over. Parker Buck getting shot wasn't meant to happen.

A hundred feet ahead, Bramwell Mace emerged from behind the root-ball of a fallen pine. He was carrying a rifle, moving cautiously towards them.

'You took your time, Bram,' yelled one of the rustlers. 'I feel like I been bit by a million skeeters.'

'Tell that to Buck,' Edson snarled.

Mace walked straight to Parker, prodded him with the toe of his boot. Reassured, he laid his rifle on the ground and started to cut his partners loose.

'You scum. You weren't meant to shoot your way back. I said to ride for the border.' Edson glared at Mace, saw the hurting in his eyes from a bullet wound in his arm. Parker must have hit him. Edson thought how much more pain there'd be if he could get his hands loose.

One of the rustlers was buckling on his gunbelt, the other swallowed tepid water from a canteen before tossing it aside.

'We goin' to ride back . . . pick up them steers?' Mace asked.

Edson's eyes blazed. 'You wouldn't want to untie me, mister,' he said dangerously. 'An' Jago Rizzle and his gunnies're closin' in. Cole Morelock ain't far behind, neither.'

'What they want you for?' Mace wanted to know.

'Murder heads the list,' Edson replied bluntly.

'An' who the hell's this?' Mace indicated Parker.

'He's a trail finder, among other things. What those might be, I ain't too sure.'

'I ain't hangin' around for Morelock,' one of the rustlers declared huffily.

'Yeah, I'm sort o' gettin' used to this freedom,' the other one said with a wry smirk.

For a minute or two, all three rustlers exchanged views. Then they looked west, walked towards where Mace indicated his own horse was tethered.

'Hey!' yelled Edson. 'What you aim to do about me an' Buck, here?

Mace sauntered back. As he cut the rope that bound Edson's wrists, their eyes met and he spoke.

'You've changed kid, but it'll come to me. It weren't so long ago I seen you.' Then he looked down at Parker. 'He's your pard ... you bury him,' he said laconically.

Edson watched as the men beaded off. He stared until his eyes watered and stung, then he saw Parker, spread-eagled in the arid dust. He'd thought the man dead, but there was a pulse, a good one. Mace's bullet had grooved a furrow in his scalp, just below the hat-rim. There was no other sign of consciousness, and there wasn't much Edson could do about patching up the wound. He looked around for his mare, knew he had to get Parker to a town and a doctor.

Sweating under the full sun, Edson tried to heave Parker up and into the saddle. But the man was awkward and a dead weight. He paused, was breathing heavily and staring into Parker's face when the man's eyes opened.

'Jeeesus,' he cried. 'Are you dyin' or what?' He sat Parker under the horse's barrel, grabbed for his canteen. It was almost empty, but he trickled the dregs into Parker's slack mouth. The trail finder spluttered and coughed, some understanding flowed back.

'Treat me gentle,' he groaned.

'I knew it would take more'n a bullet through the brain to kill you,' Edson said, unamused. He hoisted Parker to his feet and, with just a little more help, managed to get him into the saddle. He climbed up behind Parker and continued the journey to Squirrel Gap.

'I guess they took my horse,' Parker said after a few minutes.

'Yeah.'

'How about the guns?'

'They left our Colts an' a rifle, that's all. They know we ain't travellin' in their direction.'

168

Parker mumbled in response, said no more.

Every now and again Edson swung down and walked. He had to ease the burden on his mare. The sun was slanting, dipping in the west, when they staggered into the pool at Squirrel Gap. Parker, his hands seized to the saddle horn, spoke for the time in two hours.

'Off an' on, I been tryin' to figure you out, friend,' he said. 'Wonderin' why you didn't run with them hoodoo men?'

Edson helped Parker to the ground. 'Because I'm a God-fearin' honest citizen, I guess. How's your setup?'

'What you know about me's the truth.' Parker curled up protectively on his side when he got to the ground. 'Why'd you cut him loose, Edson?' he probed quietly.

Edson looked briefly unsettled. 'You wouldn't understand,' he said. 'I'm not so sure I do. Now button up . . . get some rest.'

Squirrel Gap, with its cool water and

secluded shelter, was blessed to the tired and footsore Edson. He filled a canteen and tossed it to Parker before unsaddling his grey mare. He loosed off the latigo and lifted the saddle. Then he saw a sharp, metallic flash from a break in the timberline.

A shiver ran down his spine. He shielded his eyes, held his hat against the sun's last rays to see riders edging their way along a defile in the trail. Jago Rizzle's blood bay was in the lead. Alarmed, Edson compassed the area of Snake Plain that he and Parker had just travelled through. He swallowed hard, ground his teeth in anguish. Getting away from their safe haven was now going to be real difficult.

Edson looked over at Parker, stretched out in the shade. He recalled seeing the trail finder talking to Rizzle and wondered again about their involvement. Not that it mattered any more.

'Looks like Rizzle's leadin' his riders this way,' he called out.

Parker shook off his pain, raised himself on an elbow.

'Well, you better make yourself scarce,' he said, staring at the dense shrubbery that surrounded the pool. 'Make yourself a nest in that lot.'

'An' leave you alone with Rizzle?' Edson suggested. 'I'd feel safer in a rattler pit.'

'Listen,' Parker shot back, irritated. 'I ain't in with Jago Rizzle. An' I'd be buzzard meat if not for you. You got nothin' to fear from me, cowboy. Now beat it . . . get yourself hidden.'

Edson hesitated, eyed his grey mare. 'They'll wonder about my horse.'

'Tear off one of its shoes. I'll think o' somethin'. For Chrissakes get movin'.'

Edson prised off one of the mare's fore-shoes and hurled it into the pool. He quickly estimated the distance of Rizzle and his men by a disturbed, rising flock of birds. Then he made for the brush. He used firmer ground, avoided the softer earth that could carry his imprint.

171

But in moments, beaver-tail and briar threw up a thorny, dense barricade. It was tough, painful work going forward and Edson knew he couldn't go much further. The noise he was making, together with the scampering rabbits, created a giveaway and he gave up. His clothes were ripped and his skin bloodied. He whispered soothings to the scrub jays, pleaded with them to keep quiet, hoping they wouldn't betray his position.

Less than ten minutes later a file of horsemen dismounted poolside. One of the men saw Edson's horse.

'That's the marshal's mare,' he pointed out.

Parker counted out the riders. There were four townsmen and Rizzle had three gunnies. Two of them were mountain men who rode mules. There was also a man Parker thought he'd seen before; he was wearing a deputy marshal's badge.

'Well, fellers,' Parker drawled, 'I'm real pleased to see you . . . glad you just happened along.'

Riders crowded round him, looked interested at the bloodstained neck scarf wrapped around his head.

'Where is he . . . Ringer . . . the marshal?' Rizzle asked eagerly.

'Half-way to the border if he's any sense.' Parker made to finger his wound. 'Creased me just before sunrise, then lit out.'

'Yeah? Without his mare?' Rizzle was irked, distrustful.

'It's lame . . . threw a shoe. He took my mount.'

'You know'd he was dodgin' a murder warrant. How'd you let him jump you?' challenged the Fat B owner.

'He ain't a greenhorn. You don't argue with his sort,' Parker responded. 'You think I went for this treatment?'

Impatiently, Rizzle turned away, motioned the deputy. They stood talking, low-voiced, then the lawman gathered up his posse of townsmen. They filled their canteens at the pool, resaddled and headed off west.

The gunmen hunkered beneath the bellies of their mounts, while Rizzle examined Edson's mare. It was plain to Parker that he wasn't satisfied.

'When did it throw its shoe?' he asked, walking back to the trail finder.

'I told you. Shortly before sun-up, when Ringer pulled out,' Parker told him.

'There's no wear.'

That's 'cause the dumb brute ain't been nowhere. It ain't done nothin' 'cept fill its belly with water.'

Rizzle eyed him closely. 'How come you rode out of town with Ringer? Weren't exactly a civil-minded move.'

Parker made a coughy laugh. 'I was playin' it smart . . . thought I was. I was goin' to bulldog him first chance I got. That was my mistake. Like most folk around these parts, he was too fast for me. You remember Silvy Crawle?'

Rizzle didn't respond, stood considering. Then he called to his waiting gunmen.

'Mount up. We're goin' to town.'

* * *

The party was strung out, beating an uneven trail below the timberline. Parker Buck was back astride Edson's mare, and its unsteady movement made his head pound. Sickness gripped him and he began to gag. He found it hard to remain in the saddle, clung doggedly to the horn.

The strung-out party was threading its way through a wooded pass when Parker realized that the two mountain men were missing. He felt the dread crawl over him, but with Jago Rizzle ahead and the remaining gunmen trailing behind, there was nothing he could do.

16

On Foot

Hidden deep in the tangle of brush, Edson heard the posse ride away. Then he waited for Jago Rizzle and his riders to move off to Yellow Dog with Parker. The pool was a deserted place now, and he crawled out to consider his situation. Without his horse he was dependent on the waterhole. He hunkered down, flicked small stones across the water. There was no risk of drying out, but his stomach churned at the thought of food. If Parker didn't manage to get back to him, prospects looked almighty grim.

At sundown, several cottontails made their way cautiously towards the grass around the pool. Edson took his time, slowly eased himself into a position where he could shoot. He kept his breathing shallow, his eyes half-shut. It was enough, and after ten minutes one of the older bucks got within his covering range. He swung his Colt and fired, blasted the animal's head from its body. 'Weren't goin to eat that part anyhow,' he muttered.

Skinned, the rabbit was no more than a morsel, but Edson raised a small fire and toasted it. With a handful of tiny wild onions and some liquorice shoots he dug from the water's edge, he picked at the dry flesh, sucked at the small bones.

Later, a chill breeze rolled down from the snowline of the Rafters. He built the fire up and sat close. Then he lay on soft ground, watched the moon glide from behind the mountains' ragged silver peaks. But he couldn't sleep. Instead, he listened to the rustle of small night critters around the pool, the splash of cooties, the intermittent croak of frogs. It seemed like what he'd always done.

It was long after Edson's mind had

drifted back a few years, that the croaking stopped. He raised his head, not high, just enough to see streaks of moonlight on the pool. Something was out there and had alarmed the frogs. It was something or someone they didn't know.

The fire had burned down. Its ash glowed, puffed grey and white in the night breezes. Behind the pool, the rock face rose sheer. Either side of him, lofty pine trees formed a dark barrier that was pierced by silver moonlight.

Edson shivered. There was a curious chill in the air and the quiet was intense, treacherous. He held his breath, silently wormed his way around the thorny briars towards the trees. His heart pounded from the stress; from fear of disturbing a scorpion, awakening a cottonmouth or worse.

At the back of the pool, where the first stones of the foothills formed, wild rose and broom tangled chaotically. It was a hard-to-get-to, well-camouflaged place, safe enough for the two mountain men who'd found Edson's meagre camp.

La Belle and Chater were tough and capable, but they weren't hunters of men. They were wary, learned respecters of game-quarry, and they knew about Edson Ringer's reputation with a gun.

'If *I'm* noddin' off, *he's* goin' to be dead to the world by now,' La Belle whispered hoarsely. Chater squirmed, touched the bloody scrapes across his face and neck.

'Let's hope you're right. I'll need sewin' up when I get out o' here.'

'Just try an' make less noise than a ruttin' moose,' La Belle said as they moved cautiously forward. He reached out and touched the sleeve of Chater's skin coat. 'Remember what Jago told us,' he said. 'It's five hundred between us, if we make sure. So pack him full o' lead.'

'Yeah. I'll go this way, you go that. We'll pincer him,' Chater confirmed.

Flexing fingers around their gun butts, the two men moved away; around and away from the pool towards the dying embers of Edson's fire.

But Edson was waiting under the pines, watching the dark shadowy ground that lay between him and the pool. Minutes dragged, but nothing disturbed the silence. Nothing, he thought, and blamed his stretched nerves. Maybe it was the timber-wolf returned. That would disturb the night life.

He was about to go back, rekindle his fire, when out to his left a shadow moved. He cursed silently, blinked hard. He saw it again, the low movement in the darkness. He gripped his gun, rose on one knee and fired.

The roar of his Colt reverberated wildly around the small clearing and flame seared his eyes. A harsh yell cut through the noise, and Edson fired again through the acrid tang of gunsmoke. This time, bright orange flared from Edson's right as a gun responded. Lead slammed into the tree above his head, then more gunshots crashed into the branches around him as the concealed adversary fired again.

Edson flung himself to the soft piney earth. Raincloud had started to build from the east, was scudding slow and ominous across the moon. Edson stared into the blackness ahead of him, listened for what seemed a long time, until his ears ached. Then he heard the crackle and snap of dry brush that lay beyond the entrance to the clearing. He rolled onto his side, got to his feet. The 'take it to 'em fast' tactics came back and he ran straight at the noises, held up, straightened beside the remains of his fire. He froze, listened again intently. Two horses, he thought, both of 'em kicking out for Snake Plain.

He threw brushwood on the fire and gave the embers a stir, watched it flicker back into life. A minute later the clearing was snugged in warm flickering light, closed to the outside world. Ten paces to the right, Edson saw the body of a man wearing a skin coat and leggings. But with half his throat shot away, Lou Chater had fired his last shot, wouldn't need the double-action revolver by his outstretched hand.

Edson slumped to the pool, lowered his face into the cool water, sluiced it down the back of his neck. The gunman who'd got away would be in Yellow Dog by sunrise, if that's where he was headed. That meant there'd be riders up at Squirrel Gap before noon. If he remained at the clearing he was finished. If he left it, he was at the mercy of the first rider who sighted him.

There was one chance though. If he could make it down to Goose Creek before a posse crossed it, he might get a horse from one of the valley ranches. Then he could ride north, swim the Snake River, lose himself in the Sawtooth country. If he went now, he'd have a few good hours' start. There'd be no more returning though, no settling of any old scores. It wasn't an original thought of Edson's as to why he'd jumped coach at Grey Dog.

★   ★   ★

He went higher into the timberline before cutting a trail north towards the plain and Goose Creek. The higher he climbed, the more chance he'd have of spotting the riders out of Yellow Dog. But if they managed to cut off his descent, he'd be a corpse or a prisoner before another sundown.

He broke off the heels of his boots, took a last drink at the pool and left the clearing. He saw his own dark shadow floating across the ground, wondered how long before the rain came.

It was a long haul up to where the trees broke from the first real tract of the Rafter foothills. Six years back, he thought ruefully as he rested his blistered feet, he could have made the climb easily.

He carried on for another two hours, until the very first streamers of light broke into the leadening sky. He was limping now, as he considered turning north, to find, then trail the headwater of Goose Creek.

He stayed in the trees, his boots silent on the thick carpet of mulched cone and needle. High above, the sky to the west was brightening, to the east, foreboding and dark. Edson dragged on, the soles of his feet as raw as fresh-killed meat. His legs became cramped, and his throat was cinder-dry. But a single thought sustained him; freedom, when he got to the nearest ranch and a horse.

The pine gradually thinned. Running water was ahead of him, and the ground turned to scree and shifting talus. He broke from the pine, where the headwater fell; a fast-running stream, tumbling through a narrow cleft in the foothill rock. Edson turned, looked out at the distant Snake River, Snake Plain and Goose Creek.

The face of the narrow waterfall below him funnelled up the sound. He could almost hear the soft thud of the horses' hoofs from the distant riders. He saw the flash of polished steel, the mirror-blink of a telescope, maybe.

Edson instinctively ducked, cursed. He swallowed hard against the rising panic of being trapped. Like ants, Jago Rizzle and the men from Yellow Dog moved across the land that separated the valley ranches from rising foothills. There was no refuge ahead, and he couldn't go back; back into the clutches of pursuing lawmen. No, he'd take the middle road — go down through the rock, let the stream bed take him on to the plain. He moved closer to the water, where there was a drop of nearly thirty feet, looked doubtfully at the slippery winding narrows. He was standing on the spot, while many riders were closing in. He eyed the treacherous track, took his first step.

Dread and weakness overcame him as he made his way. He felt his muscles failing, and he stumbled many times going awkwardly downwards, lost his grip against rock, grass, briar-root.

The water continued to run, fall through narrow fissures. Every now and again the rock sides went up, climbed in jagged tiers above him. He continued to move along the side of the stream, his feet painful and awkward, slipping on moss, snagging in roots. Then he came to another steep drop where the water became more of a torrent before it fell again. He took a step sideways, but his foot caught in a boulder, twisted and he pitched forward. Instinctively his body spread and his arms caught at the boulders. His fingers made a grip and he held. He was hanging and his legs thrashed as he tried to swing them up and crawl back over the edge. But he was too weak. His mind went dark and his body grew limp. Slowly his fingers loosened, gave way around the slippery stone. He fell, but his foot struck an outcrop a dozen feet below, making his body twist and turn. He hit the side of his head, before plunging into the branches of some thickly bunched alder. The trees broke his fall, and where Edson's body hit the ground it was softer, on a slope and he rolled on. He came to rest against a grassy tussock with the sound of falling water cascading in his ears; but he didn't hear it.

★ ★ ★

The cold, fresh drops of rain gathered on the leaves of the alder. Then their falling brought consciousness back to Edson's bruised and battered flesh. He tried to move, raise his head, but the pain surged through him and he was out cold again. But eventually the rain ceased and sunlight once again broke across the timberline. As the sun climbed higher it warmed the ground and awareness touched Edson's body as he lay sprawled on his back. His clothing was ripped to shreds and dry. blood smeared his legs and arms and face. His right leg was doubled under him, broken below the knee. The pain swelled, surged in his chest with every breath he took.

He stared up through the alder branches for a long time, watched the roil of falling water as it hit the rocks near his left foot. The sun was almost overhead when he moved. That would make it almost noon, about the time he reckoned to be captured, if things didn't go his way. He eased himself around a little, saw damp grass and the sweat-splattered forelegs of a blood bay. Then he looked up into the smug face of Jago Rizzle.

17

Death In The Family

In the darkness and alone, Estrella Mace thoughtfully made her way back home. She'd been to a lengthy meeting of the town's Social Committee. Nothing had been said, but the manner of those attending had spoken enough of their unease and prejudice.

But what the townspeople didn't know was, why Estrella was involved with a saloon girl. They didn't know that Jago Rizzle's frequent visits to her house were an abhorrence to her. Estrella wasn't going to tell them that she'd made a mistake; that if it wasn't for Edson Ringer, she'd have told the saloon girl to leave.

The office of the River Line night mail rang its bell for any customers to Grey Dog or towns west. Estrella wondered if she could get a seat on the coach, once again: try to leave everything behind her.

As she neared her house she saw Birdy through the unshaded windows. She sniffed and hurried onto the veranda, went quickly through the door.

'Well hello there, ain't we the *nightmare*,' Birdy murmured, chuckled.

Estrella removed her bonnet and shawl, let them drop across the back of a rocking chair.

'And I suppose you'll be waiting for Jago Rizzle?' she retorted.

Birdy shrugged, didn't answer, and neither of them spoke for ten minutes. Estrella was busying herself with impending school-work when the door was knuckled urgently. She sensed it wasn't Edson, and her heart sank.

Bramwell Mace back-stepped and stumbled, almost fell when Estrella opened the door. He stood swaying on the veranda.

'Essie. I saw you come in.' His voice was almost inaudible.

Estrella held her arms out, immediately staggered as she supported her father's weight. She brought him into the house, lowered him heavily into an easychair. In the lamplight. Estrella saw his dark, deep-sunk eyes and his grey stubbled chin, the pain etched deep across his forehead. She placed her hand on his forearm, gasped as he recoiled from her touch.

Birdy went off to fetch a bottle of whiskey that Rizzle had brought her one night.

'This is what you need, friend,' she said, with instinctive saloon patois, 'genuine wild-mare's milk.'

Mace grabbed the bottle, sucked eagerly. Then he coughed painfully.

'You got to fix this arm, Essie,' he said. 'Maybe I'll stay here . . . a few hours . . . beat it south before sunup.'

Birdy took back the bottle. 'That's enough, ol' timer. Let me see that arm.'

Tentatively, Mace pulled at a torn shirt-sleeve. Estrella found a pair of scissors and cut away the blood-encrusted bandanna. She paled at the sight and smell of the inflamed raw flesh.

'We can't heal that . . . it's rotten.' Birdy exclaimed. 'You better run for the doc.'

'No!' Mace found the strength to groan loudly, fear stark in his grey eyes. 'He'll bring that trail finder back here.'

'Parker Buck? Birdy asked. 'What's he got to do with it?'

'He caught us with the beeves . . . the herd. I shot him . . . left him for dead. But he's in town. I saw him.'

Birdy looked from Mace to Estrella, back to Mace, back to Estrella. 'Who in Lucifer's name is this old guy?' she asked, stunned.

'He's my skeleton in the cupboard . . . my pa.'

'Good God Almighty, Estrella. He's one o' them beef-stealers. If Rizzle or his men get to him, they'll string him up without question.'

'I know it, but he's my pa. I have to

get the doctor or he'll lose his arm.'

'Yeah. A few hours before his life.'

'You girls fix it up.' Mace stared up at Estrella 'That way I'll have a chance.'

'I'll clean it and put on a clean dressing. I can't do much about the pain.'

'That's all right, Essie. I'll ride south . . . sometime in the mornin'.'

'Ride under a cottonwood limb, more like,' Birdy muttered. 'I ain't ignorin' what you done, but if you tell us the story, maybe we can figure a way out. I owe Estrella that, if nothin' else.'

His voice cracked and weary with pain, Mace told of the fight in the gulch, his capture and escape. 'Can't figure why the marshal cut me loose. I remember he said he wanted favour with someone.'

Birdy sneaked a sharp, figuring-out glance at Estrella. 'That's real touchin',' she said. 'Where's your horse?'

'Tied to the fence round the side.'

Birdy crossed the room and peered from the window. While Estrella fussed, making her pa more comfortable, she went outside.

Mace had a blanket tucked around him when she returned.

'I've unsaddled your horse . . . tied it out back,' she said.

The old rustler sat up in a panic. 'Why'd you do that?'

'Because you ain't goin' anywhere for a while. It ain't far, for Chrissakes, so relax.'

Estrella turned down two oil-lamps, indicated that she and Birdy should move into the scullery.

'He's going to die, I know it. I can see the fever in his eyes. The wound's gone rotten.'

'Yeah. I know. Go get the sawbones. He'll keep his mouth shut. He's learned how to do that.'

Estrella didn't know that Mace was watching her from a window. He'd dragged himself up, his spirit damaged by the fear that gnaws at a hunted, guilty man. He gritted his teeth in agony as with one hand, he strove to pull on his boots. Eventually he left them lying on the floor, moved unsteadily across the room in worn socks. He crept from the house, moved slowly to the rear. With one hand he managed to slip on the horse's bridle, didn't even consider the saddle. He pulled himself up, and riding bareback got to the front of the house. His head lolling he stared into the night. It was the quiet and clearness that follows rain. Under a canopy of glittering stars he reeled, grunted with hurt. Then he clutched at the horse's mane, kneed the animal forward towards the street.

★   ★   ★

At the window banging, Milo Treaves pulled on his pants and tucked in his nightshirt, grabbed a scattergun that was propped in a corner of his room. He descended the stairs, heard the scurry of grain rats as he padded the length of his hardware store. He flung back the bolts and pulled open the door, saw Bramwell Mace weaving on the sidewalk.

Treaves recognized the ageing rustler. 'What the hell're you doin' here? Get away,' he snapped angrily.

Mace raised his hand. 'You got to get me out o' town. I can't make it on my own.' he rasped. 'I been hit. They'll get me . . . I ain't gettin' hung doin' your work. You got to get me away from Yellow Dog.'

Treaves cursed Mace and took a step forward. Except from a brea flare, and where yellow light from the Diggers Moon patched the sidewalk, the street was in darkness.

'Shut it. I told you never to come here,' he hissed, worried and urgent.

'You got to help me, Treaves . . . you jus' got to,' Mace raved back at him.

'I'll help,' Treaves rasped. He swung up the scattergun, cocked both hammers. Mace's eyes swivelled and his mouth opened and closed.

'No, you can't. We got to — ' he was

saying when a barrel of buckshot tore into his chest.

He flew backwards and landed on his back, found the breath to shout once more. 'We'll both die tonight, Treaves.'

Milo Treaves stood over him to pull the trigger a second time. The buckshot took Mace point blank in the neck and face. It killed him, but not before he reached his own Colt, fired just once up at Treaves.

Treaves dropped his gun, kneeled beside Mace.

'You fool,' he said quietly and fell forward across the broken, bloody body.

As the crash of the gunfire reverberated along the street, men came running. Some from the Broken Cage, some from the Diggers' Moon which was nearest.

'What happened?' one of them asked.

'Dunno,' another man said, breathlessly. 'Maybe Treaves went up against a robber. Looks like they shot each other. I guess we'll never know.'

'Yeah. The one underneath's in a mess. We'll certainly never know who he was,' the first man said, looking at Mace's body. Then he turned away uncaring and uninterested.

★   ★   ★

Estrella Mace wandered gloomily through the few rooms of her house. Absorbed in her ominous thoughts, she stared at the blanket on the floor, her pa's discarded boots. Doc Pounce had come and gone, leaving behind him the reek of warm gore and laudanum.

Birdy was trying her best at comforting when the double boom of Treaves's scattergun rolled in from the street.

The schoolteacher turned her attention to Birdy, levelled tragic eyes.

'Now he's dead,' she said wretchedly.

Birdy didn't say anything back. But she wondered, somehow thought it might be true.

Then they heard footsteps approaching the door and Estrella gasped, rushed forward at the hesitant knock.

It was Ticker Loomis, the barkeep from the Broken Cage.

'I got somethin' to show you . . . to show Miss Dove. I saw the lights on, an' I thought . . . ' he was saying when Estrella held out her hand.

'Come in. It's safer than the streets at this hour,' she offered prophetically.

No sooner had Loomis followed them inside than Birdy asked if he'd ever caught up with Slick Midland.

'Er, that's what I came up here for. You can read this.' Loomis held out a folded page of newsprint from the *Snake River Gazette*, smoothed it across his chest. 'Now I best be goin',' he said, quick and awkward while handing Birdy the sheet of paper.

When he'd gone, Birdy handed it over to Estrella. 'Here schoolma'am. You read it.'

Estrella scanned the item, summarized for Birdy.

'*Visitor to Glenn Falls badly beaten. Deputy marshal finds man lying along bank of Jackson Creek. The stranger had been savagely beaten, his features made almost unrecognizable. Papers found on his person identifed him as Slick Midland. There was no robbery, no apparent motive for the beating. Midland says he can't give a description of his assailant. After medical attention, the manager of Yellow Dog's Bull Pen saloon returned to his hotel room.*'

'Pheeew,' Birdy commented.

'Do you reckon it was *him*?' Estrella asked.

'Who, Loomis?'

'Yes. I think he was one of those with a soft spot for you. He must have known what the man did . . . to you. Perhaps he's got hidden depths of gallantry. I'd prefer to think it was poetic justice.'

'Yeah, you would. But I'll be takin' a

closer look at ol' Ticker from now on,' Birdy mused.

'Hmm. No doubt under the light of the big torch he's carrying.'

Birdy didn't follow, but she laughed. She eyed the newspaper thoughtfully, touched the still tender skin under her right eye.

'Slick played me rough, but there's a good side, you know,' she said.

Estrella shook her head. 'I would have thought not. Aren't you happy to be free of all that, Birdy?' she asked, mystified and a little despondent.

'You know what Doc Pounce says?' Birdy answered the question with another one.

'What?'

'When Slick finally cops it, he's goin' to get him buried a mile under Snake Plain.'

'Why?'

Birdy winked. 'Because deep down he's probably all right,' she jested.

Estrella thought for a second, then gave a warm, tired smile.

18

On Trial

The dog towns were almost deserted the day they tried to make judgment on Eddie Riner. It seemed that the entire population had journeyed to the county seat at Twin Falls. There wasn't an empty seat in the courtroom when the impatient judge rapped his gavel, called for silence.

Men were jostling, buzzing at the back of the court and along the walls. With three or four henchmen to escort him, Jago Rizzle was there, finely dressed, triumph gleaming in his eyes. Out of respect for her father's death, Estrella Mace wore a dark dress. If any one had cared, they'd have thought it was for Milo Treaves — Edson or Birdy hadn't let on the truth of it.

In the forefront of the court, on the

bench reserved for the witnesses, Birdy, alias Sweet Dove, was sitting. Beside her, Katey Cate, alias Mrs Rizzle, knotted and unknotted a tiny handkerchief with nervous fingers. At the end of the bench Parker Buck stretched his legs, tapped his toes together.

All eyes focused on the prisoner when he swung his crutches into the courtroom. Stories of his exploits in Yellow Dog had lost nothing in the telling, and Sheriff Cole Morelock was taking no chances. Edson had his left wrist handcuffed to the grip of his left crutch. He wore a plaster cast on his right leg, part of what Dorset Pounce had dispensed when Rizzle had brought him in.

Other than from Jago Rizzle, there was no lack of sympathy or understanding among those who watched Edson's awkward progress. There were many present at the trial who had high regard for the nerve and steady hand that had cowed Silvy Crawl and the other gunnies who'd threatened to run Yellow

Dog. A few of them had no hesitation in expressing their sentiment. Some of them remembered Ma Gracey's barefooted orphan; the boy who sought to earn his bread. Also in the courtroom sat Bo Horselip, the one-time Fat B foreman, an interested Trimmer Fogg, and the resentful Jimson Bench from Grey Dog. Rumer Wheat was there too; the sutler from Glenn's Ferry who'd accompanied Edson on their lively mail-coach trip.

Even if he had shot Bur Blackrule, some of the Goose Creek ranchers argued — and at that moment it was undeniable — the powerful cowman had asked for it. The man who'd ridden roughshod over everyone, finally got just what he'd been asking for, if not deserved. But murder was murder, and it was the sober mood of the court that reminded all of them that day. Even along Snake River, you could pay dear for lawless killing if you got caught.

Edson's bearing reflected his plight, but his eyes burned with defiance.

Flanked by armed deputies, he slumped on a hard, straight-backed chair. The courtroom was stiflingly hot and breathless, packed like a Chicago cow-pen, but Edson Ringer was chilled to the marrow.

He tried hard not to look at the faces around him. Estrella Mace had travelled twice from Yellow Dog to see him, to hand hopeful messages through the bars of the county jail. He glanced at the judge, but read nothing. He saw only a cynical, hard-bitten man, weary of renegades, killers and border trash.

He looked the jury over, twelve keen citizens whose disregard for the proceedings was an obvious reflection on their assurance of his guilt.

The county prosecutor, Lorne Parriss, was a thin, nervously alert man. He smiled indulgently, dabbed at his moist forehead, as one of the jurors removed his coat. Then he made his address. No one in the court, he promised, would be in discomfort for very long.

His premise was simple. The accused

was guilty, and that was as certain as the sun's rising in the east. He'd prove it quickly, was confident that the appropriate verdict would be returned without rile or rancour. It was simply a matter of presentation and procedure.

Had not Eddie Riner declared his guilt by an impulsive flight to who knows where? Had he not, for six years, remained a fugitive beyond the reach of United States law? Did he really believe the town had forgiven and forgotten, when he returned under the name of Edson Ringer?

But the law is not for forgiving, and it doesn't forget, the jury was told. And although the murder of Bur Blackrule had taken place six years before, the prosecutor would lay before them the findings of the coroner. He would also be calling to the stand the sole witness to the killing. The facts were irrefutable, he would ask the jury's indulgence while he presented them.

When Parriss finally got to the end of the coroner's report some feet were already scuffling with discomfort and impatience in the sweltering court-room. Most of the jury had discarded their coats, using them to pad the benches.

Sensing this restiveness, Parriss called Katherine Rizzle to the stand, got her summarily sworn in. With almost forgotten sentiment, she told how she'd witnessed the defendant shoot and kill her guardian. It was now plain however that the agitated jury were wearying. In the stultifying heat they wondered just how many nails it took to seal Edson Ringer's coffin. Due process or not, they wanted retirement, the legal formalities over and done with.

But then it was the turn of Woodley Scule; a defence lawyer from Salt Lake City. He was hired by Parker Buck, paid for by the Cattlemen's Protective. 'A curious expenditure, and probably a waste of time and money,' was how one jury member put it to another.

Mr Scule capably handled the witness, was concerned with weather conditions at the time Bur Blackrule got shot.

'Isn't it a fact,' he asked of Kate, 'that on that fateful night, a storm was raging along the Snake River . . . a storm with heavy thunder . . . incessant, dazzling lightning?'

Kate Rizzle agreed. 'Yes. It was dreadful. I'll never forget it . . . what happened.'

'And it was those dreadful lightning flashes that enabled you to see the defendant?'

'Yes . . . two or three times. I saw him clearly.'

'And did you see what weapons, or weapon, the defendant carried?'

'He had a gun. A revolver.'

'Nothing more?

'No, I don't think so? I mean no, he didn't.'

'Isn't it a fact, Mrs Rizzle, that after

the shooting . . . a month after the shooting . . . you found a Winchester rifle?'

'Yes. I found it in the creek.'

'And what did you do with it?'

'I brought it back to the house . . . put it in the storm cellar.'

'Why did you do that? Did you connect it with the shooting of Mr Blackrule?'

Immediately Lorne Parriss raised his hand, got to his feet in protest.

'All right, Mr Parriss. Proceed carefully, Mr Scule,' the judge barked.

The defence attorney smiled compliantly. 'Just tell the court why you put the rifle in the cellar?' he continued.

'I didn't want any gun lying around the ranch. Particularly after Mr Blackrule's death.'

Scule looked quizzical, raised an eyebrow. 'You didn't suspect that it might have been the gun that killed your guardian?'

'My mind doesn't work like that.' Katey Rizzle almost snapped back.

Again Lorne Parriss was on his feet with an objection.

Woodley Scule nodded amenably at the prosecutor, asked his question more subtly.

'I'm sorry. Of course, you had no reason to believe that it was the weapon that killed your guardian?'

'No. Why should I? I saw Eddie . . . Eddie Riner shoot him.'

'Tell the court when you next saw the Winchester, Mrs Rizzle,' Scule directed.

There was no more restless shuffling or indifference in the courtroom now. All eyes, including Edson's, were on the girl. Something new was emerging, and the unfolding events gripped the jury, witnesses and spectators alike. They sensed that all of a sudden, the Salt Lake lawyer was leading up to something new.

Katey Rizzle sensed the anticipation, turned square on to the jury.

'Several weeks ago,' she replied. 'Mr Buck came to the ranch. He told me that Eddie had only ever carried

210

. . . used, a .36 Whitney Colt. I was shocked . . . I didn't understand.'

Woodley Scule smiled encouragingly, beckoned with his hand for the witness to continue.

'I knew Mr Blackrule was killed by a .45 bullet. That's when I remembered the Winchester. It was in the storm shelter where I'd left it. I handed it to him . . . Mr Buck.'

From the front bench, Parker Buck wondered if Mrs Rizzle had told her husband any of that. He shot Rizzle a searching glance.

'What did Mr Buck do? Did he have a close look at the rifle?' was Scale's next question.

'He did, then he ejected a spent shell.'

The jury stiffened in their seats. the heat and discomfort now forgotten. Breathing shallowly, Jago Rizzle got slowly to his feet. He worked his way towards the side of the room where tall narrow windows overlooked the street. He looked like a man who badly

211

needed a drink, some cool air.

Parker saw Edson's eyes boring into him, diverted the look onto Rizzle.

'If the court will bear with me,' said Woodley Scule, 'I am now going to ask Edson Ringer to take the stand.'

With little discernible emotion, Edson told of his visit to the Fat B ranch and Blackrule's threat with the whip. He went on to tell how he fired at the rancher's feet as he stood on the steps, his stunned surprise when the man fell, his frightened, panic-stricken flight. He explained his long sojourn in and around the Grand Tetons, his eventual meeting with Trimmer Fogg, how he'd learned that Bur Blackrule had met his death from a .45 slug. Lastly he spoke of his return to Yellow Dog, how that became a goal to clear his name.

'You carried a Whitney .36 Colt?' inquired the lawyer, turning to face the jury.

'Yessir. I never packed anything else,' Edson said firmly, truthfully.

19

Trial's End

Parker August Buck was a trail finder with a record of service from Texas to Montana. He was next on the stand, stated that he'd been assigned by the Snake River Cattlemen's Protective to look for new, shorter trails between states. He'd also been told to look out for stolen cattle along Snake Plain. Calmly, he told of Edson Ringer's part in the gunfight with the rustlers, the former marshal's confession that he was wanted on an old murder charge, how he wanted to find the real killer.

On further questioning from Woodley Scule, he explained that on impulse, he'd ridden to the Fat B to check on Edson's story, discovered a .45 slug embedded in the porch steps.

'Was a witness present when you

discovered . . . retrieved this bullet'?' Scule asked.

'We know the answer to that,' the judge interjected. 'Get on with it, Mr Scule, before we all fry.'

Scule coughed. 'Going back to the Winchester, are you of the opinion that the shell you ejected was from the bullet that killed Mr Blackrule?'

Again, the prosecutor jumped to his feet, objecting vehemently.

Under a steely, intolerant glare from the judge, the objection was obviously sustained. But counsel for Edson Ringer's defence had made his point. Scule bowed, turned to the jury.

'This is the gun, gentlemen.' He lifted a cover from the table behind him to reveal the tarnished Winchester rifle, then turned to face the judge. 'I will be establishing later, Your Honour, that Bur Blackrule was indeed shot and killed by a .45 bullet fired from this weapon. I contend that the killer concealed it in the creek knowing full well it was incriminating evidence.'

'And how do you hope to establish that, Mr Scule?' the judge asked.

'By proving ownership, on or immediately after the fatal shot was fired. First I'd like to call Birdy Willish to the stand.' Scule leaned towards the judge. 'In Yellow Dog, I believe she's better known as Dove ... Sweet Dove,' he added helpfully.

Birdy rose, and Edson gulped because he'd never known her second name. The one-time saloon girl moved forward, settled herself in the chair beside the judge's platform.

'You tell 'em, my Sweet Dove,' yelled a dog-town local.

Again Parker looked across at Rizzle, saw the unease. Something was about to break, he sensed it.

'You are acquainted with Mr Jago Rizzle, the man who now owns the Fat B ranch?'

'Yes. I know him. We've known each other for a while.'

A gush of relieved, bawdy laughter arose from the punchers in the courtroom. But a spread of deep pink coloured Katey Rizzle's throat and a nerve-racking tick appeared in her eye.

Her shame was obvious and Birdy raised her voice to carry. 'And that don't mean what you *borrachos* think,' she lied.

But her spirited explanation wasn't enough. Even the jurymen forgot their place, their shoulders heaved and features creased. The judge pounded his gavel and frowned at the witnesses.

'Carry on, Mr Scule,' he snapped. 'And see if you can't speed things up.'

'Did the manner of this acquaintance allow for Mr Rizzle to confide in you?' the defence lawyer asked.

'Yep. Like most o' Broken Cage's barflies. Slick Midland's pop skull could run their tongues wilder than Thanksgivin' turkeys.'

Again, a mocking peal of laughter erupted from the floor.

Standing in the aisle at the side of the courtroom, Jago Rizzle fretted and fumed as the scrutiny of the men

216

around him changed allegiance, searched him out.

'The damned crib girl's lyin',' he yelled, voice thick with sudden temper.

The judge discarded the gavel, brought his fist down hard.

'Another one of those outbursts. and I'll give the guards some work to do,' he said icily. 'Continue, Mr Scule.'

Woodley Scule gave a thin, contented smile. 'Did Mr Rizzle ever comment upon the shooting of Bur Blackrule?' he went on.

'I think he said something about one man's poison bein' another's meat.'

Scule nodded. 'And did you understand what he meant by that?'

'Yep, sure did. He'd be makin' money in some way.'

There was some muttering and mumbling in the body of the courtroom. One or two of the smaller ranchers even began to shove Rizzle. At first they'd gone along with tolerant amusement, but that was now replaced by hostile suspicion. In response to

Rizzle's anxious gestures, several of his Fat B gunnies elbowed through the crush to get to his side.

But so great was the concentration of the judge and jury on the full meaning of Birdy's response that they failed to notice the disturbance and Scule continued with his questioning.

'Was Mr Jago Rizzle aware that the defendant Eddie Riner was known to you?'

'Not until later, then he dumbed up some.'

'Thank you, Miss Willish.' Woodley Scule turned to Lorne Parriss. 'Your witness.'

Parriss, who saw that his cart was losing a wheel, took over the cross-examination.

'Were there any witnesses to these alleged comments of Mr Rizzle's, Miss Willish?'

'Lordy, I hope not.' Birdy laughed. Again the courtroom erupted and for the shortest moment, a grin crossed the judge's stern-set features.

'And according to your own testimony, Mr. Rizzle was not at that time in full possession of his faculties?'

'That's right, Your Honour. He was well roostered . . . kickin' shit from the rafters.'

Again the grin appeared on the judge's face.

'Mind your tongue, Miss Willish,' he ordered. 'You're not at work now. Proceed, Mr Parris.'

'Remember you're on oath, Miss Willish. So tell the court that it's not out of any attachment . . . any long-time relationship, perhaps, to the accused, that you've cooked up these scraps of conversation.'

Birdy's lips curled scornfully. She raised an arm, pointed across the courtroom.

'I'm not a liar. What I said happened, happened. If you want more, there's the proof of it.'

Heads turned to stare at the dark-browed rancher. Rizzle glared back, his eyes glinting like those of a trapped rat.

Accepting Birdy's explicit and eloquent response, the prosecutor excused her from the stand, put Parker Buck back again.

'I understand, Mr Buck, that you took steps to establish ownership of this exhibit?' he asked, indicating the Winchester rifle.

'I did. It was sold to the son of a Goose Creek rancher. It was exactly ten days before Bur Blackrule was killed.'

'How do we know this is the same gun . . . the Winchester?'

'Each gun's numbered by the makers in Connecticut. That's who he ordered it from.'

A blanket of tension and impending dread fell across the courtroom. The only sound was the ticking of the wall clock, high above the judge's head.

'Then why not tell us all the name o' that buyer, Mister Buck,' the judge suggested.

The clock's big minute-hand clunked onto the hour, closed down the remaining seconds of the trial.

'It was Rizzle . . . Jago Rizzle,' Buck told them.

Rizzle's voice instantly screamed its denial. 'That's a lie, Goddamn you.'

'Guards, arrest that man,' the judge directed curtly and without emotion.

The two deputies stationed either side of Edson strong-armed their way into the crowd.

Now there were scuffling, snarling men threatening Rizzle. So, though now he was absurdly protected by just about everything the law had to offer, the cattlemen fought to get at him.

The judge looked on while Rizzle's gunnies threw up a reluctant defence of their paymaster. The uproar grew as the deputies clawed their way through the seething and emotional courtroom.

Then there were excited shouts as Rizzle stepped onto the high back of a bench. It was only then that Parker Buck got to his feet. He eyed the situation coolly, knew Rizzle's only escape was through one of the open windows.

Rizzle sprang upwards, his arms outstretched, groping for the broad sill. He made it, pulled one leg up, before someone lunged forward to grab his other foot. Then Jimson Bench was there clubbing from behind. The Goose Creek rancher went down stupefied and his colleagues broke apart to rush the remainder of Rizzle's gunhands. Another man hurled himself up, but Rizzle had got higher on the ledge. He was holding the window frame, kicking and stamping at the clutching fingers below him.

He tried to force himself through the open window, strove to make more of the narrow opening. But he couldn't get through the opening, and it was too late now, the surprise was gone. He looked down at the merciless faces in the courtroom, then to those who'd got to the street outside.

He moved one hand to the inside pocket of his fancy waistcoat, drew a silver-plated hideaway. He levelled it around him, centered on Edson, the man who'd brought an end to his hog-high days, his long-held secret.

But Parker was ready. 'I knew it,' he muttered as he threw his own secreted Colt to Edson. 'I owe you,' he yelled. 'Kill the miserable son-of-a-bitch. You're entitled.'

In a single movement, Edson swung his right crutch away and caught the Colt. He cursed, fell side-ways as Rizzle's first bullet smashed into the back of his chair.

'You've known for six years, you scum,' he yelled as he rolled on to the floor, grunted as the pain jarred his leg.

The guards levelled their guns, but Edson saw them.

'No,' he yelled, 'we want him alive.'

Rizzle fired again, his bullet smashing the handle of Edson's crutch, biting the handcuffs into his wrist.

'But dyin's just as natural as livin',' Edson rasped. He brought his gun up, held his breath as he met Rizzle's glare.

Both men knew Rizzle wouldn't miss a third time and Edson aimed carefully, squeezed the trigger of Parker's Colt.

'I ain't goin' for any fancy toe-shot,' he said bitterly, as he hit Rizzle high centre in the chest. Rizzle buckled from the waist. His head fell forwards, his silver-banded Stetson dropping to the ground. With one hand he loosed his grip on the window-frame, with the other he fired wildly into the roof of the courtroom. He opened his gritted mouth to say something to Edson, but he failed. His body crumpled, wheeled out and down to the ground. The men below took a fast step back, watched impassively as Rizzle's body hit the floor with a sickening thud. But like a lot of things in Rizzle's life, it didn't concern him. Nothing would ever do that again.

Edson let the Colt drop from his fingers, nodded a restrained, exhausted thanks at Parker.

'They can throw him in that grave he'd got dug for me,' he muttered.

20

Squaring Up

Edson tilted a chair back against the wall of Yellow Dog's law office, poured himself some coffee. Marshal Denver John Tilletson adjusted his feet on the edge of the cluttered, shaky table.

'There ain't many round these parts don't figure you're still the marshal,' he drawled. 'I took the job for the pay, not the rights or wrongs of it.' He slid forward in the chair, made himself more comfortable. 'I guess that don't sit too well with the town council.' He laughed. They had no choice, o' course, but now you're back, you'll be wantin' your badge.'

Edson shook his head, 'Nope,' he said. 'You hang onto it. My gun an' me are partin' ways. Comes a time when shootin' off lead don't seem a decent way to earn money. Besides, I'm sick o' bein' chased backwards an' forwards across Idaho. I'll be ridin' north when this goddamn leg mends. Montana . . . Canada even. Anywhere but west or east.'

Denver John nodded in consideration. 'Call in at the haircutters before you go,' he advised. 'If those locks o' yours get any longer, you'll be taken for Custer . . . that boy general.'

Birdy was holding court in the lobby of the Jasper Hotel. She was talking to Emmet Foyle and Johan Gries. Gathered about were two whiskey drummers, the owner of the Cactus T ranch and a few of his punchers. According to the bursts of laughter, they were all having themselves a goodly time.

Parker Buck was sitting alone when Edson dropped into the chair beside him.

'Guess I'd be jiggin' on a barrel top if it weren't for you, Parker,' he commented.

'Yeah, I guess you would at that. Me an' Kate Rizzle, that is. Now there's a missy that's had some bad luck along the way,' Parker suggested with genuine concern.

Edson smiled thoughtfully. 'I know. Reckon I might pay her a visit sometime. There's a bit that's got to be said. You know . . . square things up.' Then he changed the subject. 'Kind o' curious, Milo Treaves blastin' the lights out of old Mace?'

'Yeah, if that's what happened. Maybe it wasn't . . . quite. You spoken to the schoolma'am since?'

'No. Thought about it though.' Edson was quiet for a few long seconds. 'You figured anythin' out yet, Parker?' he asked.

'What, about Miss Mace?'

'No. I meant all the goddamn bandit stuff . . . the rustlin' . . . what led up to all this.'

Parker's brow knitted. He looked across at Birdy, tipped his hat in acknowledgment before answering.

'There's a lot o' talk that Treaves was behind all that rustlin' along Snake River,' he said. 'I'd bet my only hat it was his men holdin' up the mail-coach too. Mace rode for him, came into town for help . . . needed some proppin' up. But there'll never be any proof. They took care o' that between 'em.'

Edson recalled his journey from Pocatello with Rumer Wheat the sutler, the stage hold-up at Hognose Pass. Then he pictured Bramwell Mace; the man, among others, who fired a Winchester from a big chestnut horse.

'Do you reckon Estrella knew?' was his next question.

'Yeah, I do. She's his daughter. I reckon she followed his trail wherever he went.'

'We could get proof'

'What, ask her?' Parker half-smiled

Edson smiled back. 'No. There's still two of his cronies above ground, remember,'

'Yeah, I do now that you mention it.' The irony sounded in Parker's voice.

228

'On the safe side o' the border though . . . an' that's where they'll be stayin'.' His shoulders lifted. 'Well, none o' that concerns me. I've quit the Protective. I've had a good look at Snake River . . . ridden over a lot of it. Thought maybe I'd run me a few longhorns.' He laughed. 'It's probably safe enough now.'

Birdy broke away from her group and crossed over to join them. 'We're talkin' futures,' she said. 'You got any plans for one, cowboy?' she asked Parker.

'Nope. How about you?'

'I got a letter from Slick. He's stayin' in Glen Falls . . . openin' a new joint. He's asked me to join him. Seems like he needs me . . . can't look after himself.'

Birdy saw the incredulity, the regret in Edson's eyes as he watched quietly.

'It's my life, Eddie,' she said good-humouredly. 'I ain't up for change. You're the one that's goin' to be doin' that.'

We do hope that you have enjoyed reading this large print book.

Did you know that all of our titles are available for purchase?

We publish a wide range of high quality large print books including:
Romances, Mysteries, Classics
General Fiction
Non Fiction and Westerns

Special interest titles available in large print are:
The Little Oxford Dictionary
Music Book, Song Book
Hymn Book, Service Book

Also available from us courtesy of Oxford University Press:
Young Readers' Dictionary
(large print edition)
Young Readers' Thesaurus
(large print edition)

For further information or a free brochure, please contact us at:
Ulverscroft Large Print Books Ltd.,
The Green, Bradgate Road, Anstey,
Leicester, LE7 7FU, England.
Tel: (00 44) 0116 236 4325
Fax: (00 44) 0116 234 0205

Other titles in the
Linford Western Library:

STONE MOUNTAIN

Concho Bradley

The stage robbery had been accomplished by an old woman. Twine Fourch had never heard of a female being a highway robber before. He followed the trail all the way to a dilapidated log cabin up Stone Mountain. What happened after that no one could believe even after townsmen from Jefferson found the old log house and the skeletal dying old woman. But before the mystery could be solved there would be two unnecessary killings, a bizarre suicide and a lynching.

GUNS OF THE GAMBLER

M. Duggan

Destitute gambler Ben Crow arrives in Mallory keen to claim his inheritance, only to discover that rancher Edward Bacon has other ideas. Set up by Miss Dorothy, who had fooled him completely, Ben finds himself dangling on the end of a rope. Saved from death, Ben sets off in pursuit of Miss Dorothy, determined upon retribution. However, his quest for vengeance turns into a rescue mission when she is kidnapped by a crazy man-burning bandit.

SIDEWINDER

John Dyson

All Flynn wants is to be Marshal of Tucson, but he is framed by the territory's richest rancher, Frank Buchanan, and thrown into Yuma prison. Five years later Flynn comes out, intent on clearing his name and burning for vengeance. Fists thud, knives flash and bullets fly as he rides both sides of the law and participates in kidnapping and double-dealing. He is once again arrested for a murder of which he is innocent. Can he escape the noose a second time?

THE BLOODING OF JETHRO

Frank Fields

When Jethro Smith's family is murdered by outlaws, vengeance is the one thing on his mind. He meets the brother of one of the murderers, who attempts to exploit Jethro's grudge in the pursuit of his own vendetta. The local preacher, formerly a sheriff, teaches Jethro how to use a gun. With his new-found skills, Jethro and his somewhat unwelcome friend pit themselves against seemingly impossible odds. Whatever the outcome lead would surely fly.